"WE DO NOT INTEND TO DRAG A STRUGGLING WOMAN INTO THE STREET."

As Valonia stepped closer she raised the oddly scented package. It appeared to be a folded cloth, part of which was dangling into an old-fashioned cobalt-blue jar. "You will certainly not be struggling. And Baldric and I will be certain to take you down the back stairs. No one will see you, Guinevere Jones. Do not deceive yourself with false hope. There is no hope."

"Don't touch me," Guinevere cried. "Don't you dare touch me, you witch."

Valonia smiled evilly. "How astute of you." She lunged forward, trying to slap the cloth against Guinevere's nose and mouth. Guinevere gasped and tried to dodge. Her arm swept out in a wide, desperate arc in an attempt to ward Valonia off.

"Stand still," Baldric warned as he leapt toward Guinevere. "Stand still or I'll shoot!"

THE SINISTER TOUCH

Be sure to read the other Guinevere Jones Novels by Jayne Castle:

THE DESPERATE GAME
THE CHILLING DECEPTION

And don't miss the next Guinevere Jones Novel:

THE FATAL FORTUNE

THE SINISTER TOUCH

Jayne Castle

A DELL BOOK

Published by
Dell Publishing Co., Inc.
1 Dag Hammarskjold Plaza
New York, New York 10017

Chapter One first appeared in *The Chilling Deception.*

ISBN: 0-440-17996-3

Printed in the United States of America

October 1986

10 9 8 7 6 5 4 3 2 1

DD

Chapter One

The night had been a long one. No, that wasn't strictly accurate. It had been *lonely.*

Guinevere Jones glared at the stylish new coffee machine as it dripped with agonizing slowness. She could have bought a cheaper coffee maker when she went shopping for one yesterday if she'd been willing to settle for a plain white or beige model. But this little sucker was an exotic import, and with its dashing red-and-black trim it had totally outclassed all the bland models on the shelf next to it at The Bon. Even the glass pot was elegantly different from the ordinary coffeepot. Definitely high-tech style. She hadn't been able to resist it. It lent such a perfect, snappy note to her vivid yellow kitchen. Unfortunately it was proving to have more style than efficiency. Zac would undoubtedly have a few pithy comments to make when he tried it out.

If he ever got around to trying it out, Guinevere reminded herself resentfully as she stood in front of the coffee machine with a yellow mug dangling uselessly from one finger. Zac had been very busy with a new client lately, a client who seemed to find that the most convenient time to consult with the head of Free Enterprise Security, Inc., was in the evening. The fact that the client was Elizabeth Gallinger wasn't doing much to mitigate Guinevere's prickly mood. Guinevere's own firm, Camelot Services, which specialized in providing temporary office help, had

had a short secretarial assignment a few months ago at Gallinger Industries. Guinevere had only seen Queen Elizabeth from afar, and then just briefly, but the memory of that regal blond head, classic profile, and aristocratic posture had returned in all its glory last week when Zac had mentioned the name of his new client.

Elizabeth Gallinger was thirty-two, a couple years older than Guinevere, and already she was running one of the most prestigious corporations in Seattle. Queen Elizabeth, as she was rather affectionately known by her employees, had inherited the position of president when her father had died unexpectedly last summer. Everyone had anticipated that Elizabeth would be only a figurehead, but everyone had underestimated her. Elizabeth Gallinger had very firmly assumed the reins of her family business. Four generations of old Seattle money apparently had not led to serious mental deficiency due to inbreeding.

Guinevere was beginning to wonder if Zac was the one with the mental deficiency. If so, it couldn't be blamed on inbreeding. Zachariah Justis had a pedigree as ordinary and plebian as Guinevere's own.

Guinevere frowned at the slowly dripping coffee maker. It occurred to her that an ambitious entrepreneur with no claim to illustrious predecessors or illustrious family money might find Elizabeth Gallinger a very intriguing proposition. Zac had never been overly impressed by money, but there was always a first time.

Damn it, what was the matter with her? If she didn't know better, Guinevere decided ruefully, she might think she was actually jealous. Ridiculous. The fact that Zac hadn't spent a night with her for almost a week was hardly cause for turning green-eyed. She and Zac didn't live together. The affair they had both finally acknowledged was still at its very early, very fragile stage. Neither wanted to push the other too far, too fast. They were both carefully maintaining their own identities and their own apartments.

Fed up with the slowness of the coffee maker, Guinevere yanked the half full glass pot out from under the dripping mechanism and quickly poured the contents into her yellow mug. In the meantime coffee continued to drip with relentless slowness, splashing on the burner. Deciding she'd clean up the mess later, Guinevere hastily put the pot back onto the burner and turned away to sip her coffee.

Through her kitchen window she could see the high, arched window of the second-floor artist's loft across the street. This morning, as usual, the window was uncovered. Guinevere had never known the artist who lived and worked in the spacious, airy apartment to pull the shades. Artists were very big on light, as she had once explained to Zac when he'd had occasion to notice the tenant across the street. She smiled slightly as she recalled Zac's annoyance over the small morning ritual she went through with the anonymous man who lived in the loft.

Guinevere had never met the lean, young artist. But she waved good morning to him frequently. He always waved back. When Zac happened to be in the kitchen beside Guinevere, the unknown artist tended to put a little more enthusiasm into the wave. Zac's invariable response was a low, disgusted growl. Then, just as inevitably, he'd close the mini-blinds on Guinevere's window.

But Zac wasn't here to express his disapproval of the anonymous friendship this morning. He hadn't been here to express it for the past several mornings. So Guinevere sipped her coffee and waited for the appearance of her neighbor. Idly she studied the canvas that stood facing her on an easel tilted to catch the northern light. The young man with the slightly overlong hair had been working on that canvas for several days now. Even from here Guinevere could recognize the brilliant colors and dramatic shapes.

But there was something different about the painting this morning. Guinevere's brows came together in a new kind of frown as she tipped her head and narrowed her eyes. There was a large black mark on the canvas. From her vantage point it appeared to be an uneven square with a jagged slash inside. It didn't fit at all with the wonderful brilliance and lightness of the painting.

Guinevere went forward, leaning her elbows on the window ledge, the mug cradled between her hands. There was more than just an ugly black mark on the painting. She could see that something was wrong with the canvas itself. It was torn or slashed. Terribly slashed.

Slowly Guinevere began to realize that the huge canvas had been horribly defaced. Her mouth opened in stunned shock just as her unknown neighbor sauntered, yawning, into the brightly lit loft.

He was wearing his usual morning attire, a loosely hitched towel around a lean waist and a substantial amount of chest hair. Guinevere had decided that he always wandered into the loft just before he took his morning shower. Perhaps he had an artist's need to see how his work looked in the first light of day. He glanced at her window before he looked at his painting.

Across the narrow street his eyes met hers. Even from here she could see the questioning tilt of one brow as he made a small production out of looking for Zac. When she just stared back, her expression appalled, he finally began to realize that something was wrong. The amusement faded as his glance turned to curious.

Guinevere lifted one hand and pointed behind him. The stranger turned and glanced over his shoulder. His gaze fell at last on his ravaged canvas.

His reaction answered Guinevere's silent question of whether he had done the damage himself. The artist stood staring at the ruined canvas, his back rigid with shock. When at last he turned to meet Guinevere's eyes again, all traces of amusement had vanished. He just stared at her.

Unable to do anything else, consumed with sympathy for him, Guinevere simply stared back.

How long she stood like that, Guinevere wasn't sure. It was the artist who broke the still, silent watch. Swinging around with an abruptness that underlined his tension, he picked up a huge sketch pad and a piece of chalk. Hastily he scrawled a brief message in fat, charcoal-colored letters.

"Coffee downstairs. Ten Minutes. Please."

Guinevere nodded at once, then turned away to finish her coffee and find her shoes. She was already dressed for work in a narrow-skirted, gray pin-striped suit and yellow silk blouse. Her coffee-brown hair was in its usual neat, braided coil at the nape of her neck. She slid her stockinged feet into a pair of mid-height gray pumps and slung a leather purse over her shoulder.

Quickly Guinevere made her way through the red, black, and yellow living room with its red-bordered gray rugs and high, vaulting windows. The old brick buildings here in the Pioneer Square section of Seattle had wonderfully high ceilings and beautiful windows. When they had been gutted and refurbished, they made great apartments for the new, upwardly mobile urbanites. The busy harbor of Elliott Bay was only a couple of blocks away, and although Guinevere didn't actually have a view of the water, just knowing it was close gave her a certain satisfaction. Many mornings she walked along the waterfront on her way to her First Avenue office.

Closing and locking her door behind her, Guinevere hurried down the two short flights of stairs to the security-door entrance of her apartment building and stepped out into the crispness of a pleasantly sunny late spring morning. On mornings such as this one knew for certain that summer really was just around the corner. Another sure sign was the fact that several restaurants and taverns in the area had started moving tables and chairs out onto the sidewalks. The rain was due late this afternoon and would probably last for a while, but this morning the air was full of promise.

The missions, which were one of Pioneer Square's more picturesque features as far as Guinevere was concerned, had already released the crowd of transients, derelicts, and assorted street people that had been sheltered overnight. Without much enthusiasm the ragtag assortment of scruffy mission clients were slowly drifting out onto the sidewalks, blinking awkwardly in the sunlight as they prepared for the day's work.

Soon, either under their own power or aboard one of the free city buses that plied the short route, they would make their way toward the Pike Place Market where the tourists would be swarming by mid-morning. One particularly ambitious soul decided to practice on Guinevere. She smiled vaguely and shook her head, ignoring his outstretched palm and the request for cash as she hurried toward the restaurant.

As soon as she opened the high doors, the smell of freshly baked cinnamon rolls assailed her, reminding her that she hadn't had a chance to eat breakfast. A fire burning on the huge hearth on one side of the enormous, old brick room took the chill off the morning.

Guinevere glanced around and, when she didn't see her neighbor, decided to throw caution to the winds and order some cinnamon rolls. They arrived with butter dripping over the sides. Of course, you couldn't eat a cinnamon roll without a cup of coffee. Something was required to dilute the butter. She was paying the check when the artist slid into line behind her.

"Hi." His voice was pleasantly deep, edged with a trace of the East Coast and laced with a certain grimness. "What a way to meet. Thanks for coming. I'm Mason Adair, by the way. I feel as if I already know you."

Guinevere smiled at him, liking his aquiline features and the large, dark eyes. It struck her that he looked exactly like a struggling young artist should look. He was taller than she had thought, towering over her as she stood in line beside him. His height coupled with his leanness made him appear aesthetically gaunt. He was also younger than she had imagined. Probably about thirty. His paint-stained jeans, plaid shirt, and heavy leather sandals fit the image too.

"I'm Guinevere Jones. Want a roll?"

"What? Oh, sure. Sounds good. I haven't had a chance to eat yet."

"Neither have I." Guinevere picked up the tray.

"Here, I'll take that." Mason Adair scooped the tray out of her hands and started toward a seat in front of the fire. A few drops of the coffee in Guinevere's cup slopped over the side as he set the tray down on the wooden table. "Sorry. I'm a little clumsy by nature. Finding that canvas slashed this morning isn't improving my coordination. Shit."

Guinevere smiled serenely and unobtrusively used a napkin to wipe the cup as she sat down on one of the short wooden benches. The fire felt good even though it was produced by fake logs. Mason Adair dropped down onto the opposite bench and reached for a roll.

"I was shocked when I glanced out my window and saw that huge black square on your beautiful painting. At first I thought maybe you'd gotten disgusted with your work and had deliberately marked it up." Guinevere stirred her coffee.

"I've got a certain amount of artistic temperament, but I'd never do anything like that to one of my own paintings. Hell, I liked that one. Really liked it. I think it might have been inspired by your kitchen, by the way."

"My kitchen?"

"Yeah, you know. All that yellow. Every morning I look in your window and it's like looking into a little box of sunlight."

Guinevere smiled with pleasure at the unexpected compliment. "I'm flattered."

"Yeah, well, somebody wasn't." Morosely Mason chewed a huge bite of his roll. His appetite was apparently unaffected by his depression. "It isn't just the vandalism that got me. It was the fact that someone was actually inside my apartment, messing with my stuff. I know now why people who've been burgled say they feel as if they've been personally violated. It's a strange sensation. It gets to you."

Guinevere signed in sympathy. "I'm terribly sorry, Mason. I know it's a terrible feeling. Have you any idea who would do a thing like that?"

Adair hesitated. "No, not really. I asked you to meet me here because I wondered if you'd seen anything or anyone. I never pull the shade and you usually have your kitchen window blinds open. I thought that maybe you'd noticed something out of the ordinary last night. It must have happened last night. I was out all evening, and I didn't look at the painting before I went to bed."

"Mason, I'm really very sorry, but I didn't see a thing. I worked on some papers in my living room. I do remember going into my kitchen around nine o'clock for a snack, but your window was dark."

"No lights on?"

She shook her head. "Not then."

"Whoever did that would have needed some light, don't you think?" he asked broodingly.

"It would depend on what time during the evening he did it. It's not getting really dark until after eight o'clock now. I suppose someone could have gone into your studio and defaced your painting sometime before then and not needed any light."

Mason took another huge bite of his roll, dark eyes focusing blankly on her concerned face. Guinevere had the impression that he was trying very hard to sort out some very private thoughts. She let him chew in solitude for a moment, and then she asked, "That square that the vandal drew in black. It looked a little odd. Of course, I couldn't see it very well from my window, but there was something about the shape of it that looked awkward. Was it a child's work, do you think? Youngsters into mischief?"

"This isn't exactly suburbia. We haven't got a lot of children running around Pioneer Square. Just an assortment of street people, artists, and upwardly mobile types. All adults. At least physically. Mentally, who knows?" Mason chewed for another moment. "And it wasn't a square. It was a pentagram."

"A what?"

"A five-sided star."

Guinevere blinked. "I know what a pentagram is. What was the mark in the middle?"

"Just a zigzag slash." Mason looked down at his plate, still half absorbed in his own thoughts. "Whoever slashed the canvas must have brought along his own knife. None of my tools appeared to have been touched."

Guinevere frowned, leaning forward. "Mason, don't you find it rather odd that whoever did that to your painting chose to draw a pentagram?"

"Odd? The whole damn thing is odd. Spooky, too, if you want to know the truth."

"Yes, but a pentagram? With a bolt of lightning in the center?"

He raised dark eyes to meet her intent gaze. "I said it was a zigzag shape, not a bolt of lightning."

Guinevere hesitated. "I always think of pentagrams as being symbols of magic."

Mason didn't say anything for a long moment. "Yes," he finally admitted. "I believe they are."

There was another lengthy pause. Finally Guinevere asked, "Was anything taken?"

Mason shook his head. "No. Nothing. Didn't touch the

stereo or the paints or the cash I keep in the drawer of my workbench." He sighed. "Look, this isn't your problem, Guinevere. I shouldn't have bothered you with it."

"I don't mind. We're neighbors. Going to call the cops?"

"I'll report it, but I don't think it's going to do much good. What's a little malicious mischief these days when the cops have their hands full with real live murders?"

"Real live murders," Guinevere repeated with a trace of a smile. "I think that may be a contradiction in terms."

Mason stared at her for a second and then he laughed. "I think you may be right."

"Has anything like this ever happened before, Mason?"

His brief humor faded. "No."

"What about the possibility of jealousy? Are any of your friends resentful of your success?"

"What success? I've got my first major showing tonight, down the street at the Midnight Light gallery. I'll be lucky if someone offers me more than a hundred bucks for one of my pictures. That doesn't qualify as sudden success."

"Your first showing?"

Mason nodded. "Yeah. I just hope I live through it. I've been kind of jumpy lately, waiting for it. Whoever did that hatchet job on my painting last night couldn't have picked a worse time to rattle me. It's all I needed."

Guinevere drummed her fingers on the table, thinking. "You know, if there's anything more to this than a fluke case of malicious mischief, maybe you should do something besides just reporting it to the cops."

"What more can I do?"

"Hire a private investigator to look into the matter?" Guinevere suggested.

Mason stared at her. "Are you kidding? When I can barely pay my rent? I don't have that kind of money. Forget it. There isn't much an investigator could discover, anyway. How's he going to locate a vandal?"

"How about the little matter of how the vandal got into your studio? Was the door forced?"

Mason's brows came together in a solid line. "Not in any major way or I would have noticed. I didn't see any pry marks, and none of the locks were broken. But my apartment isn't exactly Fort Knox. It wouldn't have taken a lot of expertise to get inside. You sound like you've been watching a lot of TV lately."

"Not exactly. But I have been keeping some questionable company," Guinevere said blandly.

Mason's brows shot upward as he put two and two together. "Let me guess. That solid-looking guy with the dark hair and the super-conservative business suits?"

"Zac is trying to dress for success. He's learning the fine points of making a forceful statement in the business world while upholding the image of his firm."

"I see." Mason's dark eyes lightened with amusement. "Unlike me. How's he doing?"

"At maintaining his image? Rather well, as a matter of fact. He's just landed a very nice contract with a local firm."

Mason nodded. "So he's doing okay maintaining the image. How about in the category of making a forceful statement?"

"Oh, Zac has always had a knack for making a forceful statement when he wants to do so," Guinevere said cheerfully. Memories of Zac hunting human game on a cold and windy island in the San Juans several weeks previously flickered briefly in her head. She had to suppress a small shiver. Zac was very, very good at making forceful statements on occasion.

"I'm not surprised," Mason murmured. "I think he's made one or two forceful statements in my direction recently. The last time he closed your kitchen blinds I got the distinct impression that he would have preferred to have his hands around my throat rather than the mini-blind rod. So he's the questionable company you keep? What does he do in the business world that necessitates all this forceful-personality and image-building stuff?"

"He runs a company called Free Enterprise Security, Inc. He does security consultations for business firms."

"How big is Free Enterprise Security?"

Guinevere swallowed a scrap of her cinnamon roll. "To date there is only one employee."

"Zac?"

"Uh-huh." She grinned. "But he manages to get things done. You know, this isn't exactly his line of work, but I might mention your situation to him and see if he's got any advice. He's terribly discreet. He has to be. Businesses don't like their security problems publicized. That's why they consult outfits such as Free Enterprise Security."

Mason looked at her askance. "I have a funny feeling he's not going to be overly sympathetic."

"He has no reason to be jealous and he knows it. I've already told him that you and I have never met."

Mason chuckled. "You won't be able to tell him that anymore, will you? I can't wait to hear his reaction when you tell him you've taken to meeting me for breakfast."

Zac's reaction was forthright and to the point. He looked up in astonishment from the plastic bucket of steamed clams from which he was eating and stared at Guinevere as if she had just announced that she had made a brief trip to Mars. "The hell you did." He went back to his bucket of clams.

Guinevere pushed her own lunch aside, leaning forward to get his attention. The lunchtime crowd was heavy down here on the waterfront. She and Zac were sitting in the corner of a small sidewalk café that enjoyed an excellent view of the harbor and the tourists who were strolling the broad sidewalk that linked the boutique-lined piers.

"Zac, you're not listening to me."

"I heard every word you said." He scooped another clam out of its shell. "You claimed you had breakfast with that artist you've been ogling for the past few months. There are laws against that sort of thing, you know."

"Having breakfast with an artist?" She was getting annoyed. Deep down inside, Guinevere wondered if she'd hoped to see at least a spark of romantic jealousy inflame Zac's smoke-gray eyes. All she was detecting was irritation.

"No, ogling artists." Zac forked up another clam. "Stop trying to bait me, Gwen. I've had a hard morning. You're just mad because I had to cancel our date last night."

Guinevere set her back teeth very firmly together. "Contrary to what you seem to believe, I am not indulging in a fit of pique. I really did have breakfast with Mason."

"Mason?"

The name brought his head up again. This time there was something besides irritation in the steady gray gaze, and Guinevere wasn't sure she liked the too quiet way Zac said the other man's name. She shifted uncomfortably on the chair.

"Mason Adair is his name. He's very nice, Zac, and he's got a problem."

Zac stopped eating clams. "Is that a fact?"

"Zac, I'm serious. This morning, when I looked out my window, I could see that the painting he's been working on had been terribly defaced overnight. Someone had drawn a huge black pentagram on it and then taken a knife to the canvas. Mason was shocked. He saw me looking just as shocked and held up a sign suggesting we meet for coffee. You know, that place with the cinnamon rolls just around the corner from my building?"

"I know it," Zac said grimly.

"Well, he was rather shaken up, as you can imagine. Has absolutely no idea who could have done such a thing. He asked me to meet him on the outside chance that I might have seen something from my kitchen window. He hoped I might have spotted someone moving around in his studio last night."

Zac's gaze could have frozen nitrogen. "Did you?"

"No." Guinevere sighed in exasperation.

"Good." Zac went back to eating clams. "That's the end of it, then. No more breakfast meetings with naked artists. Hell, Gwen, I credited you with more common sense than that. You've lived in the city long enough to know better than to agree to meet absolute strangers. What got into you? Were you really that upset because I had to cancel our date?"

"I hate to break this to you, Zac, but I did not rush out to buy cinnamon rolls for a starving artist this morning just because you broke our date last night."

"He made you pay for the rolls?"

"Speaking of broken dates," Guinevere continued stoutly, "how was your little business meeting last night?"

"All business. Elizabeth is a very impressive executive. She focuses completely on the problem at hand and deals with it. Great business mind."

"Does she know how much you admire her, uh, mind?"

Zac looked at her steadily. "Are you by any chance jealous, Gwen?"

She lifted her chin with royal disdain. "Do I have cause?"

"No."

Guinevere went back to the fish and chips she had been nibbling earlier. "Then I'm not jealous." The thing about Zac was that he had a way of dishing out the truth that made it impossible to doubt him. She couldn't ignore that tingle of relief she was feeling, though. It annoyed her. "Now that we've disposed of the personal side of this discussion, perhaps we could get back to business."

"What business?"

"Well, I told Mason I'd mention his little problem to you."

"Guinevere." He rarely used her full name. When he did, especially in that soft, gravelly voice, it usually meant trouble. "What exactly did you tell Mason Adair?"

She concentrated on sprinkling vinegar on the French fries. "I just said I'd mention to you the incident in his studio last night. He's going to report it to the police, of course. But, as he said, they won't be able to do much. Just another small case of vandalism as far as they're concerned. They might even write it off as a case of professional jealousy. Mason's going to have his first show tonight. It could be that not everyone wishes him well. At any rate, Mason's fairly sure it isn't something one of his acquaintances would do. And there was something odd about that particular kind of vandalism, Zac. I mean, that business with the pentagram and the bolt of lightning in the center. It wasn't just malicious or nasty. It was weird. Pentagrams are associated with the occult."

"You're rambling, Gwen. Get to the point. What exactly did you tell Mason Adair?"

"I told you," she said with exaggerated patience. "I said I'd mention the matter to you."

"And?" Zac prompted ominously.

"And maybe see if you had any advice for him," she concluded in a mumbled rush as she munched a French fry.

"Advice?" Zac ate the last of his clams and pushed the plastic bucket out of the way. He leaned forward, his elbows folded on the table, his hard, blunt face set in a ruthless, unrelenting expression that seemed to slip all too easily into place. His dark, rough voice was softer than ever. "No, Gwen, I don't have any free advice for your starving artist. But I do have some for you."

"Now, Zac—"

"You will stay clear of him, Guinevere. You will not get

involved with pentagrams, slashed canvases, or artists who run around wearing only a towel while they wave good morning to their female neighbors. Understood?"

Guinevere drew a deep breath. "Zac, I was asking for advice, not a lecture. If you're not willing to help—"

"But I am willing to help, Gwen. I'm helping you stay out of trouble. Or have you already forgotten what happened the last time you tried to involve me in a case I wasn't interested in handling?"

"Now, Zac, you collected a nice fee for that business in the San Juans. You can hardly complain about my involving you."

"Hah. I can complain and I will complain. Furthermore . . ."

Zac was warming to his topic now. The lecture might have continued unabated for the remainder of the lunch hour if a small toddler dressed in a designer-emblazoned polo shirt and shorts hadn't come screeching down the aisle between tables and made a lunge for Zac's empty plastic clam container. The child, giggling dementedly, scrambled up onto Zac's lap, grabbed for the container, and spilled the contents across Zac's trouser leg. Empty clam shells and the accompanying juice ran every which way, splattering the restrained tie and the white shirt Zac was wearing with the trousers. There was a shriek of delight from the toddler, and then the child was racing off to wreak more havoc and destruction.

Zac sat looking after the small boy, a stunned expression replacing the hard one with which he had been favoring Guinevere. In the distance two distinctly yuppie parents ran after their errant offspring. They had the same designer emblems on their polo shirts that their son had on his. A coordinated family.

"Have you noticed," Zac asked in an odd voice, "how many small children there are around these days? Whatever happened to all those women who said they were going to have careers instead of babies?"

Guinevere tried to stifle a small grin. "I'm still keeping the faith."

Zac pulled his stunned gaze back to hers. "It's the biological clock syndrome, you know."

"Biological clock?"

"It's running out for women your age," he explained in that same odd voice.

Guinevere's grin disappeared. "Zac, what on earth are you talking about?"

"Babies," he said grimly. "My God, even Elizabeth Gallinger is talking about babies."

"Elizabeth Gallinger! Zac, what in the world were you doing talking to Elizabeth Gallinger about babies?"

But Zac was staring sadly at the clam shells strewn across his trousers. "I have the feeling this suit will never be the same."

Chapter Two

As usual disaster had struck when he'd tried to exert a little masculine authority over Gwen. Zac glanced down at the clean shirt and slacks he'd changed into at home before returning to his small office downtown. It was going to cost a fortune to have the other suit cleaned. If he hadn't known better, he would have easily believed that Gwen had summoned up the small demon child at the appropriate moment just to cut off his lecture on that damned artist.

There was more trouble involved here than just a clam-stained suit, Zac thought morosely as he opened a file labeled GALLINGER. Gwen had a knack for taking other people's problems too seriously. People liked her, they tended to confide in her. Hardly anyone willingly confided in him, Zac realized. Not unless he had the potential confidant by the throat or pinned against a wall or standing in front of a gun. Must be something in his personality that people failed to find sympathetic.

Now here was Gwen discussing pentagrams, slashed canvases, and naked artists over lunch. Zac just knew that combination spelled trouble. He had been right to instruct Gwen to steer clear of it. But, as usual, she had dug in her heels and resisted. He hadn't accomplished much at lunch, and Zac was well aware of the fact. Hell, he hadn't even arranged to see Gwen this evening. After the disaster with the clams she'd excused herself to hurry back to her First

Avenue office. Zac had been left to deal with clam-juice-stained trousers on his own.

Clam juice he could handle. He hadn't wanted to spend another evening alone, however. It had been a long week, and he'd seen very little of the woman with whom he was supposedly having an affair. Zac frowned at the notes he'd made on Gallinger Industries' security situation and wondered why labeling his relationship with Gwen as an affair hadn't made as much difference as he'd expected. Somehow, being the methodical, detail-oriented man he was, he'd assumed that putting a label on the situation would define it and cut out all the uncertainties and ambiguities. It hadn't.

What exactly had he expected? Zac wondered. That she'd move in with him? He hadn't actually brought up the subject of living together because he'd had no encouragement. Gwen had shown absolutely no interest in giving up her apartment, and she certainly hadn't invited him to move into hers. It was true he managed to spend more nights in her bed lately than he had before they'd officially agreed they were involved in an affair, but Zac still had a strong sense of uncertainty about Gwen's feelings toward him. She had never told him she loved him. He was afraid to make the assumption. Some assumptions could destroy a man.

A few weeks ago when they had returned from the island jaunt that had nearly gotten them both killed, Zac had gotten Gwen to admit that their relationship definitely had evolved into something more than a dating arrangement. At the time he had assumed the admission would settle everything between them. Instead it had only opened up more questions.

For a while there at lunch he had gotten the impression that Gwen might be a bit jealous, and in a way it had given him hope. It wasn't that he wanted her to feel insecure or hurt, but it would have been nice to know she cared enough to get jealous.

That was juvenile, Zac told himself irritably. That sort of thing was for kids, not for adults.

Adults. Gwen was thirty years old and he was thirty-six. They were both very definitely adults. For women that meant a ticking biological clock, just as Elizabeth had mentioned the other day.

Zac gazed thoughtfully across his desk. There was a glass wall opposite him, but the view was somewhat limited. It revealed only the corridor between his office and the glass-walled office on the other side of the hall. The rest of the tiny office consisted of bare walls and a small storage cabinet. Piled on top of the cabinet were the new genuine, simulated leather binders he'd ordered from the office stationery supply house down the street. Each binder was engraved with FREE ENTERPRISE SECURITY, INC. Zac thought they looked quite impressive. He would use them for presenting final reports to clients. Other than the new binders there wasn't much else to look at except the top of his desk. But he didn't notice the scenic limitations as he considered the matter of biological clocks.

Perhaps Gwen wasn't able to commit herself completely to him because she was starting to fret about the matter of babies. All around the nation women who had postponed babies for careers were reportedly starting to panic. There had been an article on that subject in *The Wall Street Journal* just the other day. Maybe, deep down, even unconsciously, Gwen, too, was getting ready to hit the panic button and decide that she wanted a baby, after all. If that happened, would she see him as good father material?

Probably not. He didn't even look like good father material to himself. It didn't take much imagination to see how a would-be mother might view him. If Gwen was getting restless because she had decided she wanted a baby, she might easily have written him off as a long-term commitment in favor of some guy who wanted sons and heirs.

On the other hand, if he was wrong and he brought up the subject of having a child, Gwen might panic for the opposite reason. She might decide that he was about to make an unreasonable demand on her. It was a decidedly tricky situation.

Zac tapped a pencil on his desktop and wondered how a simple, straightforward affair could get so complicated. The phone rang before he could come to any conclusions. With a sense of gratitude for the interruption he lifted the receiver.

"Free Enterprise Security, this is Zac Justis."

"Mr. Justis, this is Sarah, Miss Gallinger's secretary."

Zac straightened in his chair. The Gallinger account was the biggest one he'd gotten so far. He paid great attention when someone from the company called. "Yes, Sarah, what can I do for you?" He should have a secretary of his own, Zac thought worriedly. It probably didn't make a good impression on a high-level secretary from another company when she called and got right through to the head of the firm. Image. As Gwen kept telling him, you had to have a good image.

"I have a message from Miss Gallinger. She would be pleased if you would attend the cocktail party she's giving tomorrow evening. She apologizes for the short notice but assures you that she'd love to have you come. Will it be convenient?"

"Uh, yeah, sure." Zac floundered. He hated cocktail parties, but business was business. "May I bring a guest?" Gwen could handle things like this.

"Certainly. I'll tell Miss Gallinger to expect a party of two. That's eight o'clock tomorrow evening. You have the address?"

"I've got it."

"Thank you, Mr. Justis. I see you have an appointment with Miss Gallinger this afternooon at five?"

Zac winced. Another evening shot to hell. "It's on my calendar."

"Fine," Sarah said smoothly. "Good-bye, Mr. Justis."

Zac hung up the phone and went back to thinking dark thoughts about babies and biological clocks.

"Babies!" Guinevere glowered at her sister, who was sitting at a small desk in the corner. "He's been discussing babies with Queen Elizabeth. The nerve of the man. He's supposed to be having an affair with me and he's talking babies and biological clocks to Elizabeth Gallinger."

Carla flipped a handful of precision-cut blond hair back behind her ear and smiled serenely. Her beautiful gray-green eyes scanned her sister's grim expression. "You can't deny that the clock is ticking, Gwen. Elizabeth Gallinger's only a couple years older than you. It's ticking for her too. Lots of women are starting to worry, you know. They're hitting thirty or thirty-five, and panic is setting in."

"The thought of a panicked Elizabeth Gallinger boggles the mind," Guinevere said dryly. "She's beautiful, rich, and powerful. What on earth does she have to panic about? If she wants a baby, I'm sure there are plenty of well-bred studs around who will be glad to marry into the Gallinger millions."

"Perhaps she's not looking for a husband," Carla said thoughtfully. "Maybe she's only interested in having the baby. A lot of successful women are considering single parenting these days."

Gwen was stricken by a horrifying thought. "You don't think she's decided Zac is good genetic material, do you?"

"How would I know?" Carla wrinkled her freckled nose. It was the freckles that softened the exquisite beauty of her features and turned her into an approachable female. "I don't travel in Elizabeth Gallinger's circles."

"Neither do I. But Zac has been traveling in those circles a lot for the past couple of weeks." Guinevere's mouth tightened just as the front door opened. She instantly composed her face into a polite, businesslike smile. Then she saw who the caller was, and pleased surprise lightened her smile. "Mason. What on earth are you doing here? Carla, this is Mason Adair, the artist who lives across the street from me. Mason, my sister, Carla."

"I've heard all about your, er, towel," Carla murmured, gray-green eyes full of sudden humor.

"I'm sorry I can't say the same about yours."

Mason and Carla exchanged in-depth glances, and Guinevere blinked, sensing something new in the atmosphere. She ignored the feeling and motioned Mason to a chair. Men frequently reacted this way around Carla.

"What can I do for you? Have the police turned up anything concerning your slashed canvas?"

Mason yanked his eyes away from Carla and dropped into the nearest seat. "Nah, not a thing. I doubt that they will, either. That's not why I'm here. I came to invite you and"—he glanced at Carla again—"your sister to my showing tonight. It's occurred to me that there's a very good chance virtually no one will come, and with you there I'd at least have someone to talk to while the gallery owner chews her fingernails."

Guinevere smiled. "Are you really concerned that no one will attend?"

"It's happened before to artists. The other possibility is that people will show up but they'll hate my work."

Carla tilted her head. "Those are the two chief possibilities?"

Mason groaned. "Who knows? I just thought I'd try to make sure a couple of friendly faces are there tonight. Don't worry, you won't be obligated to buy a painting."

Guinevere glanced at her sister. "What about it, Carla? Want to come with me?"

"Sure. Sounds like fun. We can all stand around and sip champagne and make snide remarks about Mason's paintings."

Mason glared at her. "You've never seen my stuff. How do you know you're going to want to make snide remarks?"

"Intuition. What time are we supposed to arrive?"

He shrugged. "Sometime around eight."

Guinevere looked at him keenly. "You're really concerned about this showing, aren't you?"

"It's important to me. If it goes well, it could be a very nice break. A good start for my career."

"And if it goes badly?" Carla inquired.

"Then I go back to snitching free crackers at salad bars so I'll have enough money to buy paints and pay for the studio." Mason grinned at her. "Either that or I find myself a wealthy lady patron of the arts."

Carla assumed an expression of horrified shock. "Sell your body for money to buy paints?"

"Anything for the sake of my art," Mason intoned. His eyes narrowed as he studied her face. "Have you ever modeled?"

"Nope. And from the sounds of things you don't have enough to pay me what I'd charge if I did decide to take up the career."

"One must be prepared to make certain sacrifices for the arts, Miss Jones."

Guinevere watched the byplay closely. There was nothing surprising about Mason's immediate interest in Carla. Most men who met Carla for the first time were immediately interested. But there was something about the way her sister was responding that was a little different from usual. The sparkle in Carla's eyes was genuine, and the expression in Mason's gaze was very honest and very male. The evening ahead should prove interesting.

* * *

Mason's worst fears concerning his first gallery showing were not realized. Guinevere and Carla arrived at the Midnight Light art gallery to find that a healthy crowd had already descended on the small, discreet establishment.

"It's the free champagne and canapés," Mason explained as he met them at the door and ushered them inside. "Theresa, the owner, really went all out for me in that regard. Food really brings in the locals. Unfortunately, most of them are fellow artists, who are, by nature, freeloaders, not potential buyers. Still, it makes for a crowd."

Carla, dressed in a sweep of crinkled peach-colored cotton belted at the waist with a black sash, glanced around the room with a critical eye. "Anyone from the press here yet?"

Mason looked startled. "The press? Well, I don't know. I'm not sure who Theresa invited. The press doesn't usually pay much attention to this sort of thing, not unless the artist is really important."

"The press will turn out for free food too," Carla informed him. "But you have to get the word to them. Remind me to talk to the gallery owner later and see just who she contacted."

Guinevere grinned at Mason. "My sister has a talent for organizing."

"Oh." Mason nodded vaguely, taking Carla's arm. "Well, come on over and get some of the freebies before they're all gone." He looked around a little nervously. "I never thought this many people would show up."

Guinevere followed her sister and Mason to the champagne table, scanning the collection of paintings hung on the stark white walls. It was the first time she'd had a really good look at his work. Her previous viewings had been across the distance that separated her apartment from his studio. She had always liked the colors in his pictures, though. Through her kitchen window she'd seen canvases done in warm, vivid hues that appealed to her. But up close she realized that his work was subtly complex, the kind of painting that rewarded detailed study.

There was an abstract quality to Mason's work, but the pictures were powerful and surprisingly comprehensible. Some, such as the painting of one of the Pioneer Square missions on a cold wintry day, contained a definite social commentary. The line of men waiting for free shelter and a free meal was strangely affecting, even though Guinevere saw such lines every evening as she walked home from the office.

But other canvases were devoted to the integral play of light and color, drawing the eye with disarming ease. Guinevere liked them and found herself stepping closer to one that was predominantly yellow in an effort to read the tiny price tag.

"A thousand dollars!" She gasped. "Mason, if you sell a few of these, you won't have to eat free crackers for a couple of months."

Mason turned his head to glance at the canvas behind her. "I know," he said, not without a certain hopeful satisfaction.

"I'm glad to see the gallery owner had the sense to put decent prices on the paintings," Carla murmured as she accepted her glass of champagne. "It's important to keep the values high right from the start."

Guinevere looked at her. "I had no idea you were such an authority on the sale of art."

"I'm not. It's just common sense. Show me some of the other paintings, Mason." Carla smiled brilliantly, and Mason took her arm with a kind of stunned enthusiasm.

Guinevere found herself standing alone by the champagne table. She picked up a cracker that had a piece of smoked salmon stuck into a dab of cream cheese and wondered what Zac was doing. He'd told her earlier that he had another of his late-afternoon meetings scheduled with Elizabeth Gallinger. Perhaps they were even now discussing babies.

For the first time Guinevere wondered just how much appeal the subject would have for Zac. He'd never expressed any interest in a family life, but maybe the prospect looked more appealing to him than she'd realized. After all, he was thirty-six years old and he'd spent a lot of time knocking around the world. Maybe he'd suddenly realized he'd missed having a family. His past had been violent at times and strangely rootless. She knew his coworkers in the international security firm for which he'd once worked had called him the Glacier because of the slow but painstakingly thorough way he went about doing a job. The nickname Glacier, she had decided, could also have referred to the coldly lethal capacity he had for dealing with certain kinds of situations. Guinevere had twice seen Zac when he was on the hunt. It was a chilling vision.

But babies? Diapers? Day care? Strollers? Guinevere couldn't imagine Zac suddenly becoming fascinated with fatherhood. Unless, of course, the potential mother was the main draw. Guinevere chewed her lower lip and thought about Elizabeth Gallinger.

When she was sick of the thought of Queen Elizabeth, she picked up her champagne glass and went to study a painting of Elliott Bay at sunset. Telling herself she would not let her imagination run wild on the subject of Zac and babies, Guinevere concentrated on wishing she'd had the sense to wear something artsy such as Carla had worn. As it was, Guinevere was very aware of the fact that she was the only one in the room wearing a skirted suit and proper pumps.

"Not bad if you like sunsets," announced a masculine voice from just behind Guinevere's left shoulder. "A little trite in some respects, but this is one of his earlier works.

Mason has changed a lot during the past couple of years, and it shows in his painting, don't you think?"

Guinevere turned to face the short, wiry young man who was eyeing the painting behind her. Something about his features reminded her of a ferret. "I've just met him recently. I don't know much about his earlier work."

The man smiled with an air of superiority. "I see. You're new on the scene around here?"

"If you mean new on the art scene, the answer is yes. I'm Guinevere Jones."

"Henry Thorpe." He waited impatiently for some sign of recognition, and when it didn't come, he frowned. "I've had a couple of showings here, myself, but I guess if you're new in the art world, you wouldn't have known about them."

"I see." One of Mason's freeloading fellow artists, Guinevere decided. There was a certain nervous energy about Henry Thorpe that she found curious, almost unnatural. It was as if he were operating at a higher internal speed than most of the others in the room. Perhaps Henry Thorpe indulged in other substances besides free champagne. Anything for the sake of art.

"You don't look like you're here for the free food," Thorpe announced, scanning her neat suit. "So I assume you're a potential buyer?"

"I'm very interested in Mason's work," Guinevere said politely.

"Yeah, so are a few of the others," Thorpe said slightly grudgingly. "I guess it's the superficial accessibility of the stuff. People who don't know much about art like it because they think they can understand it."

Detecting more than a small measure of professional jealousy, Guinevere deliberately turned back to study the painting of the bay. But Henry Thorpe edged closer.

"You'd never guess it from that sweet little painting of sunset on the water, but ol' Mason wasn't exactly a sweet character when he did that picture. He was running pretty wild a couple of years ago. Hung out with a weird crowd."

Guinevere frowned. "Mr. Thorpe, I'm really not interested in hearing this."

"If you want to buy a painting from a guy who used to run around with witches, that's your business. But personally I—"

"Witches!" Astonished, Guinevere swung around to confront Henry Thorpe. Memories of a black pentagram flashed into her head. "Witches? What on earth are you talking about, Mr. Thorpe?"

Sensing that he may have blundered socially, Thorpe tried to back off. "Oh, well, it was no big deal. You know how it is. People sometimes get mixed up in strange things, and Adair was pretty strung out a couple of years ago. Had a bad time with his family back East, and I think he tried to forget his problems by getting involved in something really off-the-wall. But that's all over now. I mean, it's not like he would have painted hidden symbols of the occult into these canvases or anything. You don't have to worry about that."

"What doesn't she have to worry about, Thorpe?" drawled Mason Adair as he came up behind the smaller man. Carla was still firmly tucked into his grasp.

"Nothing, Mason," Thorpe assured him hastily. "Just talking about some of your paintings. Not a bad crowd tonight. Any buyers?"

"Most people seem to be here for the same reason you are," Mason said, assuring him smoothly. "The free champagne."

Thorpe risked a cynical smile. "You can't hold that against us, friend. You've been known to hit a few showings for the free food yourself. Excuse me." With a nod for both women Henry Thorpe slipped back into the crowd.

Mason watched him go with a wry expression. "He's right, you know. I have made a few meals off a showing like this. Can't blame the others for turning up tonight. I just hope they don't elbow all the potential buyers aside in their lunge for the food."

"I don't think you have to worry about that," Carla said with a certain satisfaction as she watched the gallery owner hang a SOLD sign on a painting across the room.

Mason followed her gaze and whistled silently. "Jesus. Theresa put a price of fifteen hundred on that sucker."

Guinevere grinned. "Congratulations. You're going to have something to celebrate when this is all over." And then, remembering the comment Thorpe had made about Mason's past, she couldn't resist adding, "Your family will be excited." The reaction was immediate and grim. Mason's expression of dazed pleasure vanished beneath cold, hard lines.

"My family," he said far too calmly, "can go to hell. That's where they sent me." Then he saw the concern on Carla's face and made an obvious effort to shake his suddenly savage mood. "Hey, forget it. It's no big deal. My family and I don't exactly communicate these days. My old man wrote me off the day I made it clear I was going to make a career in art instead of law. That's old history. Let's get some more champagne."

Several more SOLD signs went up before the evening ended. A certain subdued excitement had infected the crowd. Theresa, the gallery owner, was bubbling over with heady enthusiasm as she darted about, answering questions. By the time he and Guinevere had put Carla into a cab to send her back to her Capitol Hill apartment, Mason's mood was euphoric. He stood on the sidewalk until the cab was out of sight and then started walking Guinevere back to her apartment building. It was nearly midnight and the streets were empty.

"Hey, it went okay, didn't it?" Mason said for what must have been the fiftieth time. "It really went okay."

"It went better than okay," Guinevere said, assuring

him. "You heard Theresa. She's ecstatic. You're all set, Mason."

"Are you kidding? This is just the beginning. There's no such thing as being all set in this business. Every new painting gets judged against all the others you've done. But at least I've proven I can sell. Dad never thought I would get this far, you know."

"Didn't he?"

"Hell, no, he—" Mason broke off abruptly. "Forget it. I don't want to talk about him. Not tonight."

"How about witches, Mason?" Guinevere asked gently. "Want to talk about them?"

He stopped short and stared at her under a street lamp. "Witches! You mean that stupid pentagram business?"

"Mason, that man, Henry Thorpe, said something about your once having been involved in some kind of occult group. And that damage to your painting last night looked pretty vicious. If there's any possibility of a connection, don't you think you ought to tell the police?"

Mason muttered something that sounded quite disgusted. "Thorpe. God knows what he was running on tonight. He hasn't been able to paint decently for almost a year and it's eating him alive. What did he tell you about witches?"

"Nothing much. Just that for a while a couple of years ago you'd been mixed up with some sort of odd group."

Mason shoved his hands into the pockets of his leather jacket. "Yeah, it was odd, all right. But it wasn't dangerous. Bunch of folks sitting around playing games with stuff they learned out of old books. For a while it was just a friendly group that met to get a little high on some homegrown agricultural products and have a few laughs. An excuse to party. A couple of the members started taking things too seriously, though, and I got out. So did almost everyone else. The partying was getting in the way of my painting."

Guinevere frowned, considering. "You don't think there's any possibility of a connection between what happened last night and that group?"

Mason shook his head impatiently and resumed walking. "Not likely. Most of the people I knew who were part of the crowd have long since dropped out. Like I said, it was just an excuse to party. I haven't seen any of the original group for months."

"Where did you do all this, er, partying?"

"One of the members, a guy named Sandwick, had inherited an old house. Mostly we used it. Had a spooky old basement that was soundproof. Neighbors couldn't hear us if we got too loud, not that the neighbors would have cared. It wasn't exactly a high-class area."

"Where was it located?"

"Near Capitol Hill." Mason sounded totally uninterested. "Let's talk about something more to the point."

"Such as?"

"Such as your sister, Carla."

Guinevere smiled. "As I told you, she's an organizer. She used to be an executive secretary, but lately she's been working for me."

"Is she free?"

"No, actually, she can be quite expensive," Guinevere remarked, remembering certain incidents from her sister's recent past.

"Come on, Gwen, you know that's not what I meant."

"All right. She's not involved with anyone special at the moment. Does that answer your question?"

"It does."

"There's just one other thing, Mason," Guinevere went on slowly. "Please excuse the big-sister spiel, but I'm afraid it comes with the territory. I *am* her big sister and I don't want her hurt. She went through a bad experience a few months back. She's over it now, but I wouldn't want anyone undoing all the progress she's made." Carla's "progress" had cost a bundle in therapy, Valium prescriptions, and patience. It had also led directly to Guinevere's first meeting with Zachariah Justis. That first encounter had been very unnerving. It had taught her right from the start that Zac could be quite ruthless.

Mason grinned. "You do sound like a big sister. But don't worry. I'll take good care of Carla. If she'll let me."

"Be prepared to be organized."

"I can't wait." Mason stopped in front of Guinevere's security door. "Here we are. I'll walk you up the stairs like a good Boy Scout. I really appreciate you and Carla coming to the gallery tonight. I was not exactly cool and calm ahead of time, and it was good to know there were going to be some friends there."

"It was a very successful evening, Mason. You should be proud of yourself." Guinevere dug her key out of her shoulder bag as she climbed the second flight of stairs.

"Relieved is the word, I think." He waited, lounging against the wall, while she slipped the key into her lock. "Well, good night, Gwen, and thanks again for showing up tonight." Mason straightened and turned to start down the stairs.

"There seems to be something wrong with the door." Guinevere pushed tentatively against it. "I was sure I left it locked. I always lock it."

Mason paused, glancing curiously back over his shoulder. "Anything wrong?"

Guinevere shoved open the door and stood looking into the living room. "Nothing you can do anything about, Mason. Good night." She closed the door very gently in his face and turned to confront Zac.

Zac put down the glass of tequila he had been holding and leaned his head back in the chair where he had been sitting for the past two long hours. The expression in his ghost-gray eyes made Guinevere think again of glaciers.

"I think," Zac said in a voice that showed all the rough

edges, "that we have a communication gap here." He got up out of the chair and came forward with grim delibera-tion. "You and I are supposed to be having an affair. That, for your information, implies exclusivity. What the hell do you mean by coming in at midnight with that goddamned artist?"

Chapter Three

"I'm not an errant wife coming home late after a night on the town," Guinevere managed to say in a surprisingly even voice. She wasn't feeling at all even inside. She'd never seen Zac in quite this mood. There had been times when he'd been annoyed with her and she'd seen him concerned and had been around him when his temper grew a little short. But she'd never seen such blatant anger and outrage.

"No, you're not an errant wife, are you? You're a bored mistress coming in after a night on the town."

Guinevere's head came up with a snap. Furiously she tossed her shoulder bag down onto a black leather chair. "Don't you dare call me your *mistress,* Zac. A mistress, for your information, is a kept woman. And you don't keep me, Zac Justis. Lately you haven't even kept me company!"

"So you decided to go out and find someone else to keep you company?"

"It's none of your business what I did tonight." She was moving farther and farther out on the thinnest possible ice, but her own anger was in full sail. "You have no right to yell at me like this."

"No right? You come home at midnight with that naked artist in tow and you tell me I don't have any right to yell?"

"He wasn't naked."

"How long would it have taken him to get naked after you invited him into your apartment?"

"I didn't invite him in, not that it would have made any difference. Mason walked me home after his gallery showing tonight. He invited Carla and me to attend. Since I didn't have anything else to do tonight and since he's a very nice person, I decided to accept the invitation. I had a couple of glasses of free champagne and half a dozen salmon canapés. I resisted the impulse to buy one of his paintings. Primarily because I couldn't afford one. That, Zac, is the sum total of my wild night on the town. Mason and I left the gallery about fifteen minutes ago, and I can produce witnesses if necessary. Is there anything else you'd like to know?" Summoning up a courage she wasn't sure she actually felt, Guinevere walked right past Zac, flung herself down onto the black sofa, and glared across the room at the egg-yolk-yellow floor-to-ceiling bookcase. She refused to glance at Zac, who was watching her the way a predator watches its prey.

"Yes, goddammit, there are a few other things I'd like to know. Were you planning on inviting him in for a nightcap? What's his view of the evening's entertainment? Is it as charmingly innocent as yours?"

Guinevere swung her gaze from the bookcase to Zac's glittering gray eyes. "Mason is falling rapidly for my sister. A typical male reaction around Carla. She's about all he talked about on the way back here this evening. Now, if we're going to discuss innocent evenings, why don't we dissect yours? How long did the after-work session with Elizabeth Gallinger go? Did you find it necessary to conclude your business over dinner and a few drinks? Did you go to her place or yours after that?"

Zac ran a hand through his dark hair, his expression turning frustrated. "My meeting with Elizabeth was all business."

"Really? No more chitchat about babies and biological

clocks?" His eyes narrowed quickly, and Guinevere knew she'd struck gold. "Oh, I see. The subject did arise, then? Before or after you gave her your analysis of Gallinger's security needs?"

"You don't know what the hell you're talking about. I left Elizabeth several hours ago, went home, and started trying to call you. I thought you might be in the mood for a late dinner. When you failed to answer your phone for over two hours, I finally decided to come over here and make sure everything was all right."

Guinevere couldn't stand the way he was starting to pace back and forth in front of her. The movement reminded her too much of a stalking cat waiting to pounce. Uneasily she kicked off her pumps and got to her feet. She walked past him, ignoring his glare, went into the kitchen, and turned on the light. The mini-blinds were raised and she could see that Mason hadn't yet let himself into his apartment. The studio window was still dark. Guinevere reached for the teakettle. She didn't feel like waiting for the new coffeepot to crank through its elegant ritual. Zac appeared in the kitchen doorway as she switched on the burner.

For a long moment they looked at each other without saying a word. With a woman's instinct Guinevere knew that some of Zac's initial fury had cooled.

"Everything was just fine, Zac. There was absolutely no need for you to be concerned. We don't have to account to each other for every moment, do we? We're having an affair. We're not married. The simple truth is that Carla and I spent a pleasant evening at the gallery. Mason walked me home afterward. That's all there was to it." She kept her tone quiet and remote.

He was silent for a moment. "I discussed business with Elizabeth and then went home and started calling you. That's all there was to my wild evening too."

"I don't like being called your mistress."

"I'm sorry. Lately I've been feeling"—he paused—"possessive." His gaze was steady. "What should I call you?"

"The name is Gwen. You don't have to use any other labels." She turned away to reach for a couple of mugs and saw the light come on across the street in Mason's apartment. There was no sense adding new fuel to a fire that was starting to die out, Guinevere decided. Catching sight of Mason through the kitchen window would probably not set well with Zac. Out of sight, out of mind. She put the mugs down on the counter and went to lower the blinds. Her hand was on the cord when an abrupt movement in the studio caught her eye.

"Zac!"

He was at her side instantly. "What is it?"

"Zac, there's someone in Mason's studio. Oh, my God, look!"

Mason had sauntered into the high-ceilinged room, automatically turning on the lights. A dark, hooded figure, who had apparently been inside the apartment when Mason opened his door, dashed across the floor, hand upraised. From their vantage point Guinevere and Zac could make out Mason's startled reaction, and then the hooded figure was upon him.

"Call 911." Zac was already on his way out of the kitchen, heading for the front door.

Guinevere reached for the phone, punching in the short emergency code. With her eyes riveted to the drama taking place across the street, she quickly gave the address and situation to the person on the other end of the line. "Just hurry, will you?" she snapped when the dispatcher patiently asked for her name and address as well as that of the victim's.

Guinevere slammed down the receiver and leaned forward, staring out the window. She could see Mason's crumpled body on the floor. The hooded figure was straightening slowly. Some instinct must have warned him that he was being watched. Turning, the man glanced out of the studio window. For a taut moment his gaze locked with Guinevere's.

She couldn't see much, Guinevere realized as she frantically tried to take mental notes. The hood fell forward around his face, hiding almost all of the details one was supposed to recall in this sort of situation. Besides, she was too far away to make out such things as the color of his eyes. But she could see the heavy line of the jaw, and there was a certain sense of bulkiness under the old shirt and pants he wore. A heavy man. She was almost positive she wouldn't be able to identify the man if she ever saw him again, though. Frantically she tried to find some unique feature. The hood, itself, was the oddest part about him. It was shaped like a cut-off monk's cowl. It shadowed his face and fell into a short cape around his shoulders.

As they stood facing each other through the windows it occurred to Guinevere that the cowled man had as good a view of her as she had of him. Belatedly she reached out and turned off her kitchen light.

But the man in Mason's apartment was already swinging around in alarm. He must have heard Zac's footsteps on the stairs. Or perhaps seeing Guinevere had jerked him into action. Whatever the trigger, it sent him running out of the apartment.

Helplessly Guinevere watched as Mason's attacker fled. With any luck he might run into Zac on the stairs, she thought. But a few seconds later Zac burst through the door and went straight to Mason's prone figure. There was no sign that Zac and the cowled man had tangled.

Guinevere raced across the kitchen and out her front door. At the last minute she remembered she wasn't wearing any shoes. As she grabbed a pair of sandals out of the closet she heard the first police sirens in the distance. She shoved her feet into the sandals and hitched up the narrow skirt of her suit. Then she was running down the two flights of stairs to the street. Out on the sidewalk she dashed toward the entrance to Mason's building. The security door was propped open with a copy of the Seattle Yellow Pages that belonged on the shelf beneath the pay phone in the small lobby. Zac's work, Guinevere assumed. Perhaps to make access quicker for the cops. She wondered how he'd gotten inside the security entrance so quickly. But Zac had a way of doing things like that.

She flew up the stairs to the second floor and glanced down the old, linoleum-lined hall. Mason's building hadn't been as expensively renovated as hers. In fact, it looked to be in what was probably a sadly original condition. The dim halls and shaky banister on the staircase made the place look a little like a cheap hotel. At the opposite end of the hallway there was a faded exit sign, indicating a fire escape. If Zac hadn't met the escaping attacker on the staircase, it was probably because the man had used the other exit.

The door standing open at the end of the hall had to be the one to Mason's apartment. Guinevere rounded the corner just as the sirens whined into silence outside the building.

"Zac! Is he all right?"

Zac was crouching beside Mason. He didn't look up. "He'll live. Whoever it was got him on the side of the head, but the blow must have been deflected. He's groggy but not unconscious. Did you see any sign of whoever it was who did this, Gwen? I didn't pass him on the stairs."

"I think he must have used the fire escape. I got a brief glimpse of him through my window while I was dialing 911."

Zac did glance up at that, pinning her with grim eyes. "Did he see you?"

"I . . . I think so, but he must have heard you about that time and dashed out of the room. He was wearing a weird hood, Zac. It was very strange." Guinevere broke off as footsteps echoed on the old stairs.

"I'll handle this," Zac said, getting to his feet.

Guinevere nodded obediently. Zac was good at this sort of thing too.

On the floor Mason groaned and opened his eyes. "Hell of a way to celebrate my first show."

It was a long time later before Guinevere found herself alone with Zac back in her apartment. She was tense and troubled. Zac sprawled on the sofa, eyeing her as she stalked back and forth in front of him.

"I don't understand it, Zac. Why didn't Mason tell the police about that incident with his painting last night? Damn it, he told me he'd filed a complaint. Or at least he implied he was going to file one. But tonight he didn't mention it. Instead he acted as if he'd just been unlucky enough to walk in on a routine burglary this evening. He didn't try to relate the two incidents."

"I didn't hear you rushing to fill in the missing pieces," Zac observed quietly. "You didn't say a word about that pentagram or the canvas slashing, either."

Guinevere threw up her hands in frustration. "Because I could see Mason looking at me, practically begging me to keep my mouth shut." She turned to glance at Zac accusingly. "And you went right along with Mason's limited version of the story too. Why?"

Zac shrugged. "The same reason you did, I suppose. It was pretty damn obvious Adair didn't want to link last night's incident with tonight's, and even more obvious that he'd never mentioned the slashed canvas to the authorities. I could see him watching me as I talked to the cops, and I knew he wanted me to say as little as possible."

"So you did."

"I told them what I'd seen through your window tonight, which wasn't much. Hell, I didn't even get a look at the guy. He was long gone by the time I reached Adair's apartment."

"But you knew about the pentagram and the slashing," Guinevere reminded him.

"All right, so I decided to respect Adair's wishes and keep quiet about it. I'm used to dealing with clients who prefer not to involve the cops. I guess it's getting to be second nature to abide by the client's wishes."

That much was the truth, Guinevere thought. Many of Zac's business clients had no desire to see their company's name dragged through the newspapers or to have any association at all with criminal activity, even though they were the victims. That's why they hired discreet security firms such as Free Enterprise Security, Inc. Precisely so that such unpleasant matters would be handled *discreetly*.

"Are you saying Mason is now a client?" Guinevere asked brightly.

Zac glared at her. "No, I am not saying that. I merely made the point that I'm used to working for people who don't want the police involved. Out of habit I respected Adair's wishes tonight. That's all there is to it."

Guinevere sighed and sank down onto the opposite end of the sofa. "I wonder what this is all about, Zac."

"Beats the hell out of me." One arm draped along the back of the cushion, he continued to watch her closely. "But whatever it is, I don't want you involved. I've told you that before, Gwen. I mean it."

"Zac, Mason's a friend."

"I thought he was just a ship passing in the night."

"Well, it's more a case of a permanently anchored ship. With a porthole that looks straight into my porthole."

"I've been aware of that for some time," Zac drawled. There was a short silence. "I heard him tell the cops that he'd been to the show at the Midnight Light gallery tonight with you and Carla."

"So?"

Zac exhaled heavily. "I shouldn't have chewed on you earlier this evening."

"Is that an apology?"

"Yeah."

Guinevere risked a small smile. "I shall treasure it always."

"You do that. I don't apologize very often."

"I know."

There was another short pause before Zac said promptingly, "Well? Don't I get one too?"

"An apology?"

"You owe me something for all those not-so-subtle accusations about the meeting with Elizabeth."

"I guess I do. I know she's an important client for you, Zac. And I'm a businessperson. I understand about client demands."

"So when do I get the apology?" he pressed.

"I thought I'd already given it!"

"No," he said, leaning forward to haul her onto his lap, "you haven't. But you will."

Her mouth curved tremulously as she automatically braced herself with one arm around his broad shoulders. "Going to exact your pound of flesh?"

"And then some." Zac brushed his mouth against hers, sampling her lips with easy, possessive familiarity. His large palm spread warmly across her thigh. "You have such nice flesh."

Guinevere relaxed against him, luxuriating in the welcoming heat and strength of his hold. Her fingertips lost themselves in his thick, dark hair. He murmured something sexy and outrageous into her ear.

"What was that?" she demanded, pulling slightly away.

"I said I adore the pink perfection of your rose-colored lips; that the column of your throat reminds me of a Grecian statue and I could kiss the ground upon which your dainty feet tread."

"Funny, that's not what I thought you said." She tugged at the first button of his shirt.

"Okay, so it lost something in the translation. Let's not quibble."

"Wouldn't think of it." She slipped her fingers inside the white shirt and found the dark, curling hair on his chest.

His hand tightened on her thigh, and he began unfastening her silk blouse. When the delicate garment fell unheeded to the gray rug, Zac groaned softly and kissed her shoulder. "I've missed you lately, sweetheart."

"Not as much as I've missed you." She snuggled more closely as he undid the front catch of her bra and pushed it off her shoulders. When his palm rubbed gently across her nipple, she closed her eyes and let her fingertips sink into his chest.

"Do you know what you do to me when you respond like this?" Zac lowered his head and put his mouth on the crest of her breast.

"Ummm." She could feel the rising need in him. Under her thigh he was growing heavy with desire. His immediate response was every bit as exhilarating for her as he claimed hers was for him. Their physical attraction for each other had been intense and immediate right from the start. But as their relationship deepened into a full-fledged affair it seemed to Guinevere that the physical side of things was changing, growing more complex and variable. Vaguely she wondered why it should be that way. It was as if there were more questions now than when they had first started making love, questions they hesitated to ask each other.

"We both have too many clothes on," Zac muttered as he slid his hand down her side to her bare waist and found the opening of her skirt.

"Do we?"

"Definitely." He surged to his feet, lifting Guinevere in

his arms, and strode toward the bedroom. "But I think we can handle the problem."

He finished undressing her in the shadowed bedroom, his hands gliding over her with a hunger that was building rapidly in its intensity. Guinevere struggled briefly with his slacks, but he grew impatient and unsnapped them himself. As the last of their clothing fell away Zac eased her down onto the bed, pushing apart her legs so that he could lay comfortably between her thighs.

"You're in a hurry tonight," she teased, her eyes gleaming.

"It's been too long." He ducked his head to kiss the hollow of her throat. Deliberately he let her feel him poised at the damp, silky opening of her body. "I'm a creature of habit, Gwen. And lately I've gotten into the habit of going to bed with you as frequently as possible. You can't just cut a man off from his habit without a few serious consequences. I've been suffering withdrawal symptoms for the past week."

"It's your own fault you've been suffering," she couldn't resist pointing out.

"Don't remind me. I finally get an evening that's at least partially free, come rushing over here, and what do I find?"

"No more lectures, Zac."

He sucked in his breath as he felt her lift her lower body against his with tantalizing emphasis. "No," he agreed fervently. "No more lectures." He caught her shoulders and eased forward, just barely entering her. He waited eagerly for the small intake of breath that told him she was reacting as passionately as she always did to his possession. Zac ached with need, but he had grown addicted to that first little gasp with which she always greeted him and he always held himself in check until he heard it. When he felt her nails dig lightly into his shoulders, he surged forward, burying himself in the tight, clinging warmth.

"Ah, Zac. *Zac.*"

Her passion made him forget all that had happened that evening. It wiped out the memory of the long nights he'd been spending alone lately, and it obliterated the jealousy that had gripped him earlier. At this moment she was completely his once more, and he thrived on the knowledge. Thrived, hell. It made him feel complete and alive and filled him with a satisfaction that nothing else could equal. Zac reveled in the mental sensation just as thoroughly as he gloried in the physical. There had never been any other woman who could do this to him.

His body drove into hers, setting up an inevitable cadence that could only lead to one conclusion. Guinevere's eyes were closed as the passion crystallized within her. He could feel the strong, feminine muscles in her thighs as she wrapped her legs around his waist and held him close. She wanted him as completely as he wanted her, and Zac knew he would cheerfully kill to keep her in his arms.

When he sensed the delicate tightening that signaled the beginning of her climax, Zac fought the familiar battle to restrain himself until she was so far along the path that it would be impossible for her to turn back. Then, when the little shivers gripped her, he surrendered to his own pounding desire, a stifled shout of triumph and satisfaction mingling with her small cries.

Zac waited a long time before rolling reluctantly to one side. He felt pleasantly exhausted. Guinevere lay cradled inside the curve of his arm, and he idly toyed with the nest of damp, dark hair below her flat stomach. Her lashes lifted with lazy, lingering sensuality as she looked up at him.

"Apology accepted?" she asked throatily.

"Hell, yes. I'm not an unreasonable man."

"Hah." She grinned and tickled him.

"Watch it," he advised, not bothering to move.

"Why?"

He groaned. "Why is it you always have so much energy after we do this, while I'm always in a state of total exhaustion?"
"Don't whine about it. Just a basic constitutional difference between male and female. It's not your fault men have this fundamental weakness."
"If we're weakened so much afterward, it's only because we have to do all the hard work."
"Excuses, excuses." She leaned across him, folding her arms on his chest and resting her chin on them.
"Speaking of excuses . . ." he began slowly as he remembered something.
"What about them?"
"I wasn't able to think of any to get myself out of a cocktail party tomorrow night. A business thing. Will you come with me so I don't have to stand in a corner by myself?"
"Luckily you've caught me in a generous mood. Who's giving the party?"
There was a slight pause before Zac said quietly, "Elizabeth Gallinger."
Guinevere deliberately allowed herself to pause before responding. She thought she could feel Zac tightening a little beneath her. "Received a royal summons?"
"Something like that. She's a good client, Gwen. I don't want to offend her. At least not until she's paid for the analysis I've been preparing."
"That much I can understand. And since I definitely don't want you standing alone in a corner all evening, I'll be gracious and go with you."
"You're too good to me."
"I know." She drummed her fingers lightly on his chest and grinned wickedly. "Much too good to you."
"Fortunately for me," Zac murmured, ruffling her hair, "I don't let humbleness cripple me."
"I can see that." One of his legs moved between hers,

and Guinevere was suddenly aware of a resurgence of the throbbing heat that had consumed him earlier. Her fingertips slipped down his rock-hard belly to the stirring shaft of his manhood. "I thought you were exhausted."

"I am. This time you'll have to do all the work." He reached down and gripped her waist, lifting her lightly and settling her on top of him. "Show me how much energy you've really got."

Guinevere sank down along the length of him, a secret, sensual smile curving her mouth. "More than enough for both of us," she promised him softly.

Guinevere woke the next morning to a muttered expletive that reached her all the way from the kitchen. She blinked slowly and peered at the clock. Almost seven. Usually she was up and moving by six. Last night Zac had been determined to make up for several lost evenings. As she stretched, she felt the results in the muscles of her thighs.

"Where in hell did you get this stupid excuse for a coffee machine, Gwen?"

She groaned and pushed back the covers as Zac's shouted question reached around the corner into the bedroom. "Don't yell, you'll wake the neighbors."

He appeared in the bedroom doorway, two mugs dangling from his left hand. He was already dressed, his hair still damp from the shower. "You chose that sucker for its color, didn't you?" he accused. "It was the red and black trim that seduced you. You can't resist anything bright when it comes to decorating this place, can you? Do you realize that at its present rate of production that coffee maker is going to take an hour to produce two cups of coffee?"

"Possibly, but it will be really terrific coffee, Zac. Trust me."

"I'll bet you didn't even bother to research coffee machines before you went shopping for one. I should have gone with you. At least I could have kept you from buying some off-brand piece of junk."

"You're wrong. It's not off-brand, it's imported." She got up and reached hastily for her robe. There had been several mornings now when Zac had seen her rising naked from a tangled bed, but she still wasn't accustomed to the way he watched her when she was running around nude. "And I did research coffee machines. But when I got to the display at The Bon, this one just stood out from all the rest. It was as if it had 'Buy Me, Guinevere Jones' written all over it. I couldn't resist it. It's beautiful."

"It's a disaster."

"Details, details." She finished tying the sash of the robe and smiled brilliantly. "Relax. It'll have the coffee ready in a moment. I'm going to take a shower."

"Maybe we'll have one mug of coffee out of that idiotic device by the time you're dressed, but I wouldn't count on it." The phone rang in the kitchen, and Zac turned away to answer it.

Guinevere traipsed after him. It was, after all, her phone, her apartment, and her kitchen. Zac had a way of assuming a lot of rights around the place on the mornings after he'd spent the preceding nights. She'd seen this syndrome previously. When she reached the kitchen, he was already speaking into the phone.

"Okay, Gertie, I'll take care of it right away. Thanks for the message." He replaced the receiver and glanced at Gwen. "That was my new answering service."

Guinevere smiled contentedly. "I'm glad you took my advice and hired one. Answering machines don't leave the best impression on clients. Much better to have a human answer your phone when you're out. How did Gertie, or whatever her name is, know to call here?"

"I left this number with her last night." Zac busied himself with the toast that had just popped out of the toaster.

"I see." Guinevere considered the implications. Zac had obviously intended to spend the night when he'd arrived the previous evening. Well, she could hardly hold his rather arrogant assumption against him. After all, they were involved in an affair.

"Want a bite of toast?"

Guinevere nodded. "So who was the message from?"

"Elizabeth Gallinger. She wants to see me first thing this morning." Zac was taking great pains with the buttering process. "Breakfast meeting."

Guinevere gritted her teeth and forced herself to smile sweetly. "Oh, good. You won't have to worry about getting coffee out of my new machine. *Liz* can buy you a cup."

With a certain air of defiance she glanced toward her kitchen window, but there was no view into Mason Adair's apartment this morning. Zac had lowered the blinds.

Chapter Four

Carla glanced up disapprovingly as Guinevere walked into the office that morning. "You're late." Then she added with great interest, "Did Zac spend the night?"

"It occurs to me, sister dear, that your extensive interest in my social life is due to the fact that you're bored. I don't think you've got enough to do around here now that you've got all of Camelot's files in order. Your skills as an executive secretary are being wasted." Guinevere hung up her umbrella. It was a myth that Seattle residents never carried umbrellas, a myth perpetuated by the locals, who liked to pretend that they were indifferent to the misty rain that was a major factor in their environment. Hers hadn't been the only umbrella out there on the street this morning, and there was no way those others could have belonged to tourists. It was only eight o'clock. Most self-respecting tourists were still in their motel rooms at this hour.

Carla gave her sister a strange glance. "I thought you appreciated me getting your office organized."

Instantly Guinevere was sorry she'd made the comment. From the force of long-established habit she backed off, not wanting to hurt Carla's feelings. But damn it, she told herself, it was time Carla was out on her own again. Besides, Guinevere wanted her office back, even if she might not run it quite as efficiently as Carla did. "You know I've been extremely grateful for all the work you've done. It's just that now you have everything down to such an efficient routine that I'm beginning to feel like an unnecessary accessory around my own office. It's time you took on a new challenge, Carla." She waved a hand around the room, indicating the sum total of Camelot Services' headquarters. "This place is just too small for you. You're trained for bigger and more exciting things. You're too skilled, too much of a professional, to continue working here as a clerk."

Carla's mouth trembled a little. "I'm not sure, Gwen. I just don't know."

"What I need is part-time clerical assistance," Guinevere said gently. "Hiring a skilled, executive secretary such as you to work here is like hiring a Thoroughbred race horse to pull a wagon. I've got a dozen people in my files who can handle the clerical work required by Camelot Services. You should be out earning big money and managing an executive office. Carla, you mustn't let that incident at StarrTech keep you from going back to the kind of work you were trained to do."

Carla's beautiful eyes were wary and wistful. "I know, Gwen. It's just that I've felt, well, safe here."

"I realize that. But you're also getting bored here. You were born to organize someone or something."

"You don't get bored here," Carla pointed out.

"I own the place. It may be humble, but it's mine." Guinevere smiled. "It makes a difference, you know."

Carla sighed. "All right, I can take a hint. I'll start keeping an eye out for another position."

Instantly Guinevere was stricken with guilt. "There's no rush, you know. We can watch for something interesting that might come through Camelot Services. Lots of times people ask for short-term, temporary secretaries whom they then wind up hiring as permanent staff."

Carla's insipient depression disintegrated beneath a

wave of humor. "I know. And you chew nails every time it happens."

Guinevere was pleased to see how quickly her sister had thrown off her bad mood. A few months ago such a mood might have settled on Carla for a full day or more. Her sister really was back to normal, and it was time she went back to the kind of work she liked. "Well, it is a little irritating to have some of my best temps stolen, but I guess it goes with the territory. Besides, it's good advertising in a way. The people who get full-time jobs tell others how they landed them through Camelot Services, and the new employers are impressed with the quality of the people we send them. You have to look on the positive side."

"I'm glad you're feeling so positive and philosophical this morning, because Bonny Hatcher's husband just phoned to say Bonny went into labor last night and had her baby at three this morning."

Guinevere stared at her. "But she wasn't due for another couple of weeks!"

"These things happen, Gwen. Healthy baby girl. Seven pounds, two ounces."

"Good grief. Zac was right?"

"About the sudden onslaught of baby making?"

Guinevere nodded dolefully. "It's scary, isn't it? Everyone is either talking about babies or having them. And you read all the time about how well all those new fertility clinics are doing. It's the latest fad among educated, successful women. Biological clocks. Probably just a craze, but when it's all over, there are going to be a lot of kids running around."

"Oh, my God," Carla breathed. "You are really starting to worry about this, aren't you?"

"My imagination has been running riot a lot lately." Guinevere pulled a stack of folders toward her as she sat down at her desk. "But business comes first."

"Wait a second," Carla said bluntly, "What about Zac? How does he feel about the new fad of having babies?"

Guinevere opened a folder and stared unseeingly at the contents. "I don't know," she said quietly. "I just don't know."

Carla grimaced. "Haven't the two of you talked about the subject?"

"Not directly."

"But, Gwen—"

"Look, Carla, I don't have the answers to your questions, so let's get down to work. As long as you're sitting at that desk, you might as well do something useful. Get on the phone and see who you can find to replace Bonny Hatcher at Fogel's today. She was due to work there for another five days to replace his secretary who's on vacation. We can't let Fogel down. He's been a small but very loyal client." She glanced at the clock. "His insurance office doesn't open until ten. That gives us less than two hours."

"I'll find someone. I can always go out myself if necessary." Carla reached for the phone and the folder full of temps who were qualified for Fogel's kind of office.

"Oh, and Carla, when you're finished, you'd better send flowers to Bonny's hospital room. And maybe one of those little designer baby suits."

Carla chuckled. "A designer baby suit?"

"Don't laugh. It's what the new brand of baby is wearing these days."

"Okay." She started to dial.

"And when you're finished," Guinevere added deliberately, "I've got something important to tell you about Mason Adair."

Half an hour later, as Guinevere finished her story of the events in Adair's studio, she was glad she hadn't brought up the subject until after Carla had located a replacement for Bonny. Carla nearly went into shock.

"Good Lord! Is everyone all right? What about Mason?"

"He's okay. He got a few bruises in the struggle, but he wasn't badly hurt. He refused to go to an emergency room."

"And you and Zac?"

"We're fine," Guinevere assured her. "It was probably the sound of Zac racing up the stairs that drove off the intruder."

"I've got to call Mason." Carla was already dialing.

"I don't see why," Guinevere began calmly, only to be interrupted by Carla as she spoke urgently into the phone.

"Mason, what's this I hear about an intruder in your apartment last night? I can't believe it. Are you all right?" Pause. "Are you absolutely certain? There can be delayed effects from this sort of thing, you know." Another pause as she listened to Mason. "Yes, yes, I realize that, but all the same—" Long pause while Carla listened impatiently. "I know, but I still think you should take it easy today. What do you mean, you can't? Just don't try painting until tomorrow. There's no sense pushing things. Besides, you deserve a break after your brilliant show last night." Carla frowned. "Oh, I see. I didn't realize. Your cousin? Well, I'm not sure. After all, this is your family and all, and I know there are problems. I wouldn't want to make things awkward." One more pause. Carla suddenly seemed to change her mind. "I understand completely. Of course we'll be there. One o'clock. Yes, I know the restaurant. See you then, Mason."

Guinevere leaned back in her swivel chair and eyed her sister. "What on earth was that all about? Where, exactly, are we going to be at one o'clock?"

Carla appeared to remember something. "You're not already scheduled for lunch with Zac, are you?"

"Zac didn't schedule me in for anything today," Guinevere said dryly. "He left my apartment in a big hurry. Had a hot breakfast meeting with Liz. My next appointment with Zachariah Justis is tonight. I'm due to escort him to the queen's party. Zac was afraid that if he went alone, he'd be a wallflower. Fat chance. I'm sure Ms. Gallinger would have found some way of entertaining him."

"Gwen, I hate to tell you this, but you're losing your objectivity. Are you jealous?"

"Of course not. Forget that and tell me what's happening at one."

"Mason's cousin is in town. Just showed up without any notice. Called Mason's apartment this morning. He's been sent here on family business, apparently. He's taking Mason to lunch, and Mason doesn't wish to be alone with his cousin. Feels it will be a stressful situation, to say the least. I volunteered you and me to run interference. The lunch is free, Gwen. Cousin's going to pick up the tab."

Guinevere eyed her sister appraisingly. "Carla, haven't you learned yet that there is no such thing as a free lunch?"

"What could go wrong?" Carla asked with perfect confidence.

"We could become embroiled in an embarrassing family conflict."

"Nonsense. By going we'll be helping Mason to avoid a conflict."

Guinevere gave up the argument and went to work.

Dane Fitzpatrick turned out to be something of a surprise. He was, according to Mason, the son of his father's sister, an only child, just as Mason was. Apparently the family had always expected Dane and Mason to be close friends, but the truth was, they had very little in common. When they were very young, Mason said, there had been a distinct hostility between himself and his cousin, probably promoted by the fact that the other family members tried to force them to be buddies. But there were also some very basic differences between the two men. Dane had been content to fulfill family expectations as far as career and lifestyle were concerned. Mason had been of a more independent and rebellious temperament.

Given Mason's surly comments on his cousin, Guinevere wasn't expecting the gallant, charming, thirty-five-year-old man who looked as if he had just stepped out of a fine East Coast law office. Impeccably dressed in a gray suit and old school tie, his slightly thinning hair meticulously trimmed, Fitzpatrick exuded quiet confidence and the sense of authority that came naturally to those who are descended from a long line of successful upper-class lawyers and a good family. He was a handsome man, with the kind of physique that spelled tennis courts, golf, and sailing on a regular basis. He had what must have been the family's dark eyes, judging from the fact that Mason had them too. He also had excellent manners. Guinevere was surprised by the gracious way he covered up his astonishment at seeing Mason walk into the restaurant with two strange women in tow.

"Please sit down," Dane said with quiet gallantry as he accepted the introductions. "Mason, you should have mentioned you were bringing guests. But no matter. This table will seat four."

Guinevere glanced around at the interior of the expensively paneled restaurant. The place was noted for its fish, of course, just as most of Seattle's good restaurants were known for seafood. But this particular restaurant was also known for its prices. It looked as if it had been established for fifty years, but Guinevere knew for a fact that it had been built only recently. Nevertheless, the mahogany walls, old-fashioned chandeliers, and heavy green carpeting gave the impression of a much older heritage. She had been looking for an excuse to dine here, and she wondered now whether Mason or his cousin had chosen the place. A waiter materialized near Dane Fitzpatrick.

"Would anyone care for a drink?" Fitzpatrick asked.

"Sure," Mason said. "I'll have a beer."

Mason hadn't bothered to dress for the occasion. He was wearing his usual paint-stained jeans, a scruffy-looking pullover, and an even scruffier pair of Nikes. There was a certain air of defiance about him that touched Guinevere. She had the feeling that Mason had been battling his family a long time. Carla was watching him with a protective expression, as if ready to jump between Mason and Dane, should violence erupt. But violence wasn't about to erupt, Guinevere knew. Dane Fitzpatrick would never stoop to such blue-collar behavior. Above all, he was a gentleman.

"Well, Mason, I had planned to discuss business with you, as you well know, but since we have guests . . ." Fitzpatrick let the sentence trail off. His meaning was clear. This was family business and not meant for the ears of outsiders.

"Don't worry about Carla and Gwen. I've already told them why you've flown three thousand miles just to take me to lunch. You can talk in front of them."

"Perhaps they would prefer that we didn't," Fitzpatrick suggested with grave politeness. It was obvious he was seeking a socially acceptable path out of an uncomfortable situation.

It was Carla who took charge of the conversation at that point. She buttered a chunk of French bread and said blithely, "Did you hear about Mason's show last night? Very successful launch. Several important paintings were sold, and next time there will be press coverage. He's on his way in the art world."

Fitzpatrick looked directly at Mason, who was nursing his beer. "I'll be sure to tell your father."

"Why bother? Dad could care less. But he must have been the one who sent you out here on this wild-goose chase. You wouldn't have come on your own. Why, Dane? What's happening back home to make him suddenly start wondering how things are going with the black sheep of the family? And how did you get my address? I haven't communicated with anyone back East for nearly two years."

"Your father asked me to try to find you, Mason. It's taken quite a while. When I told him that I had a Seattle address for you at last, he asked me to come and see you. You know him. He's much too proud to contact you himself. As it so happened, I had business out here on the Coast. After I finished meeting with my clients in L.A. I flew directly here. I think you should consider it an overture, Mason. Your father is a stubborn man. He'll never be able to bring himself to contact you first. Not after what happened between the two of you. But this is his way of trying to tell you the door is open."

"But I'm the one who's supposed to take the big step and apologize? What good would that do, Dane?" Mason asked wearily. "An apology isn't going to solve the problem. As far as my father is concerned, nothing will solve the problem except for me to give up trying to make a career out of my painting. You know as well as I do what kind of life-style he thinks I'm living out here. As far as he's concerned, I'm beyond the pale. Decadent, addicted to God knows what, and totally immoral."

"Mason, perhaps you should give the old man a chance," Fitzpatrick said earnestly. He appeared to have forgotten Guinevere and Carla now, as the conversation came down to brass tacks.

"What chance did he give me or my painting? He drummed me out of the family the moment he found out that I was absolutely serious about art. Forget it, Dane. Go back home and tell my father that I haven't changed my mind."

"Your father's will—" Fitzpatrick broke off with an uneasy glance at the two women. Obviously this was too important to discuss in front of strangers, regardless of Mason's lack of concern.

"I don't give a damn about my father's will. I know I'm out of it. But I just don't give a damn. You're welcome to enjoy every penny, Dane."

"Mason, it doesn't have to be this way."

"Yes, it does," Mason said stonily. "The only thing that will ever change it is if the old man admits I have a right to live my life the way I want to live it. What do you think the odds are that he'll do that, Dane?"

Fitzpatrick sighed heavily. "Not good. He's a stubborn, willful old man who has ruled the family for too many years to back down now. He'll never accept your art. You're right about that. If you come back, he'll still want you to give it up."

"Sending you out here to see me was just one more maneuver to try to coax me back into the fold, wasn't it?"

"You're his son," Fitzpatrick said. "It's natural he would try to bring you home."

"On his terms."

"As I said, he's a very stubborn man."

Mason put down his beer mug and glared at the older man. "Tell my father that unless he's prepared to accept me for what I am, I'm never coming home. Not after the things he said to me two years ago. He's the one who threw me out, Dane. There's no way I can come back until he takes the first step. Having you stop by and take me to lunch doesn't constitute a first step as far as I'm concerned."

Dane Fitzpatrick seemed to accept the fact that he had done his duty and that it wasn't going to have any major impact on Mason. He nodded sadly and summoned a deliberately charming smile for Guinevere and Carla. "I fear we are ruining lunch for your friends, Mason. Let's change the topic."

"Good idea." Grimly Mason signaled for another beer.

Guinevere sensed Carla's silent sympathy for the brooding young artist and sent her sister a commiserating glance. All things considered, it was an awkward situation. She hoped her other social engagement of the day would fare better, but she had her doubts.

At ten o'clock that evening Zac found himself exactly where he had feared: standing in a corner alone, drinking tequila. Guinevere was here, all right, but not at his side. She had been easily snagged by a small knot of women her own age, and from what he could overhear of the conversation, they were all discussing babies. He couldn't tell if Gwen was participating enthusiastically or just keeping up her end of the conversation in order to be polite. He wished he knew. If Baby Fever was striking her, he wanted to know about it and be prepared for it.

From the shelter of his corner Zac watched Guinevere as she chatted with the others. He always took a certain possessive satisfaction in watching her. Tonight she had her dark hair in its customary twist at the nape of her neck. The style looked businesslike when she wore a suit, and absolutely elegant when she wore the kind of thing she had on tonight. He liked the fact that she wore her hair up during the day and on social occasions. It lent a certain intimacy to the act of taking it down for bed. Zac was aware of a fierce possessiveness as he thought about taking the pins from Guinevere's hair later on tonight.

The red silk dress was scooped at the neckline, gracefully full in the sleeves and bodice, and pulled in snugly at the hips. Zac had liked the feel of the material under his palm earlier that evening when he'd guided her into Elizabeth Gallinger's beautiful Mercer Island home. It had made him think of how good Gwen's skin felt when he was making love to her.

Zac took another swallow of the tequila and decided he probably shouldn't get started thinking along those lines.

This was a business party. The last thing he wanted to do was embarrass himself in front of Elizabeth Gallinger's wealthy guests. If he wasn't careful, he'd have to go hide behind a potted palm. It still amazed him that Guinevere could so easily affect him. Tonight, after the party, he would take her home and then to bed. He could wait. She was his for the evening. His for as long as he could hold on to her.

Zac just wished he knew how long that was likely to be. There was still a strange element of uncertainty in his relationship with Guinevere Jones. It worried him primarily because he didn't know how to go about fixing the problem. Zac was accustomed to solving problems. He might be a little slow at it, but he was thorough. It annoyed him that this one wasn't getting resolved. How the hell did she really feel about him? How committed was she to the affair? And just how interested was she getting in babies? He looked around the room, and all he could see were two dozen biological clocks dressed in evening gowns. It was a daunting image. Maybe he'd had a little too much tequila.

Across the room, prominently displayed over a white couch, was a Mason Adair painting. Guinevere had spotted it the minute she'd walked into the room. It was a canvas full of life and interest, a study of an old woman reading a book. For some reason, although there was a wealth of aging character in the face, the feeling projected by the painting was of youthful discovery. Even Zac, who admitted to himself that he knew next to nothing about art, could feel the effect of the painting.

"I've heard that Queen Elizabeth prides herself on being a patron of the arts. She enjoys 'discovering' the best and the brightest of the new talent. I saw a lot of good stuff on display in the lobby of Gallinger Industries when I worked there for a while a few months ago. It's a real coup for Mason Adair that she obviously thinks enough of his work to have a picture hanging here in her home. I wonder if he knows she bought one?" Guinevere had commented in low tones when they had walked into the glass-walled living room. She had then given him a brief résumé of her experiences at lunch with Mason and his cousin, Dane Fitzpatrick, describing how alienated Mason was from his father. Before Zac could tell her he didn't approve of her having lunch with Mason Adair, Elizabeth Gallinger had come gliding across the room to greet them.

Now, as Zac stood contemplating the picture in greater detail, a soft, throaty voice made him glance to the side.

"Ah, Zac, there you are. I've been looking for you." Elizabeth Gallinger swept through a cluster of her guests who parted for her automatically. Elizabeth had that effect on people. She was a very beautiful woman who projected the kind of self-confidence that came from old money and old family. Zac couldn't imagine her giving a party that was anything less than an unqualified success. Everyone she invited would come. What had Guinevere called such an invitation? A royal summons. But then, Guinevere had been acting strangely whenever Elizabeth's name came up lately.

"Hello, Elizabeth. Looks like a great party." Zac winced inwardly at the inanity. He wasn't sure what else to say. It was easy enough to discuss security matters with Elizabeth Gallinger, but on any other topic he simply couldn't think of much to say. What did you talk about to a woman who moved in Elizabeth's circles if you weren't talking business?

"You don't appear to be enjoying yourself," Elizabeth complained, her crimsom fingertips settling lightly on his jacket sleeve. "What happened to that nice Guinevere Jones?"

"She's talking to some of the other guests." Zac glanced across the room. Guinevere still appeared to be trapped in the baby discussion. Either that or she was staying in it of her own free will. He wished to hell he knew which.

"Oh, yes, I see." Elizabeth smiled with great charm. "It's getting a little stuffy in here, don't you think? What do you say we go out onto the patio for a few minutes?"

Zac looked at her in mild surprise and then nodded. "If that's what you'd like. Sure."

"Once this kind of party is up and running, no one really needs the hostess," Elizabeth confided lightly as she led the way out of the white-and-pastel living room. The royal-blue bodice of her gown was sequined and cut to reveal a surprising amount of cleavage. For some reason the look was elegant on Elizabeth. Not at all tacky, Zac decided. Just the same, he wouldn't want Guinevere wearing anything like that out in public. Elizabeth's blond hair moved around her face as if it had been privately trained by her hairdresser. Until now Zac had only seen Elizabeth Gallinger in French designer suits. It didn't surprise him that she looked just as at home in what was probably a French designer gown.

They stepped through a pair of open French doors and out into the cool evening. The rain had disappeared shortly after noon today, and the temperature had immediately climbed into the low seventies. Some of the pleasant warmth still lingered although it was fading rapidly. Elizabeth walked over to a teak railing and leaned against it to gaze out over a discreetly lit garden. Acres of sloping lawn stretched down to the waters of Lake Washington. Across the expanse of dark water the lights of Seattle and Bellevue glittered.

"A lovely evening, isn't it, Zac?"

He nodded again and then realized she might not be able to see the affirmative motion because of the shadows. "Very nice." God, he was a stunning conversationalist. It wasn't like this with Guinevere. He had no trouble at all talking to her. And she had no trouble talking to others. It was one of the reasons he'd wanted her with him tonight. She could keep a conversation going. Unfortunately she was wasting her talent in a discussion of babies this evening.

"I've been extremely pleased by your analysis of Gallinger's security needs, Zac. Now that the project is almost concluded, I want you to know that I'll be recommending you to other people in my position."

"I appreciate that, Elizabeth."

"We've spent a lot of time together over the past few weeks. I feel as though I've gotten to know you quite well," Elizabeth continued in a thoughtful tone.

Zac, who didn't feel he knew this woman at all well, except as a client, tried to find something neutral to say. "It's been an interesting project."

She was silent for a moment. He could see her perfectly chiseled profile as she continued to gaze out into the garden. "On occasion during the past few weeks I've found myself talking to you about a subject I haven't discussed with anyone else, Zac. Something about you made me think you would understand."

Zac froze. Babies. She was going to bring up biological clocks agin. He knew it. Where was Gwen when he needed her? "Uh, well, Elizabeth, I'm sure a lot of women are discussing the same thing these days."

She swung around, a smile curving her perfect mouth. "You see? I knew you sensed what I was getting at. I've made the decision, Zac. I'm going to have a baby. I'm going to become a single parent."

He cleared his throat. "That's terrific, Elizabeth. I'm sure you'll make an excellent mother."

"Oh, I will," she assured him serenely. "I'm in a position to give a child everything. And I will. But the most important thing I can give my baby, Zac, is good genes. My own are impeccable. But I must make certain the father's are equally sound."

Zac felt his mouth go dry. "Genes." He didn't know

what else to say, but he could feel a wave of panic unfolding in his stomach.

"I don't intend to marry, of course. There's no need for that at this point."

"I see."

"But I will certainly expect to pay well for the services of a good father. I want the best, Zac. I can afford the best."

Zac took a step backward and found himself up against a wall. His tie was suddenly much too tight around his throat, and it seemed to him that the night air had become almost unbearably warm. Behind him he could hear the laughter and the careless conversation floating through the French doors, but safety was a million miles away. "Elizabeth, I think I'd better go find Gwen. She doesn't know too many people here tonight, and I shouldn't leave her on her own."

Elizabeth stepped closer. Her perfume was filling the air, making it difficult for Zac to breathe. He hated perfume. One of the things he liked about Guinevere was that she never wore any.

"You needn't worry about your relationship with Miss Jones," Elizabeth said soothingly. "I only need you in one capacity. It can be our little secret. Once the job of impregnating me has been done, I won't have any further need for you."

Images of black widow spiders popped into Zac's head. He was aware of a definite dampness under his armpits. Hastily he downed the last of the tequila. In his lifetime he'd faced armed men, scheming swindlers, and fanatic terrorists. But Elizabeth Gallinger was a first. He was almost immobilized by the experience. Gwen, he yelled silently. Gwen, do something! Aloud he said in as cool a tone as possible, "Miss Gallinger, I believe there's been a misunderstanding here."

"Would it be so unpleasant, Zac?" she asked with the

confidence of a woman who knows she can have any man she wants. "I'd want to do it the natural way, of course. I don't like the idea of artificial insemination. My attorney will handle all the details, including the cost for your services. I assure you, you won't have any complaints." She took another step closer and raised her face invitingly.

And then, just when Zac assumed all was lost, Guinevere's voice came liltingly across the patio.

"There you are, Zac! I was wondering what had happened to you. I've been looking everywhere." She came forward easily, smiling at Elizabeth. But Zac could see the unnatural glitter in her eyes. "Have you forgotten we have to be home by eleven? Elizabeth, it's been a wonderful party. Thank you so much for letting Zac bring me along. Fabulous view from up here," she added, waving at the lights that ringed the lake. As she reached Zac's side she put a hand possessively on his arm.

Zac rushed to accept rescue with the same alacrity with which wagon trains used to greet the cavalry. "Of course, Gwen. I was just saying good night to Elizabeth. The security work I'm doing for her firm is almost finished, you know. It's been quite a project." He put his arm around Guinevere's waist and turned to smile politely at Elizabeth Gallinger. "It's been a great party. I'll see that the final report on Gallinger Industries' security needs is on your desk by Friday. Have your secretary contact me if there are any questions. Ready, Gwen?"

"Ready. Good night, Elizabeth."

"I'm so glad you both were able to come," Elizabeth was saying with automatic graciousness. But she didn't get a chance to finish the farewell. Zac and Guinevere were already halfway back to the French doors. A moment later they disappeared inside the elegant living room.

Five minutes later they were climbing into Zac's aging Buick and heading toward the floating bridge that linked Mercer Island with the city of Seattle. Nothing was said until he was parking the car in front of Guinevere's apartment house. It was obvious, Zac realized, that if he didn't break the fraught silence, no one would.

"I have never," he growled as he opened the security door, "been so embarrassed in my entire life. I couldn't believe what I was hearing, Gwen. I couldn't believe it. From a *client,* no less."

Guinevere said nothing. She was already on the second-floor landing, inserting her key into her lock. Zac reached out and took it from her to finish the job.

"She wanted me to stand at stud for her, Gwen."

"Can you do it standing up? You must show me sometime."

"Gwen! Listen to me. This has been one of the most unnerving nights of my entire life. You have no idea what it was like. The woman assumed she could buy my *genes.*"

"Are they for sale?" Guinevere marched through the open door, her back ramrod straight.

"Gwen, don't do this to me. You've got to understand what happened back there." Zac hurried through the door, closing it quickly behind him as he struggled for words to explain the ordeal he had just lived through. But whatever words he might have found, died forgotten as he saw Gwen's sudden stillness. She was staring across the room at a blank wall. "Gwen? What the hell . . ." Instantly he was moving forward, looking for the source of her shock.

Abruptly Zac remembered that there had been a large mirror hanging on that wall. It lay now in huge, jagged shards on the floor. Someone had pushed the broken pieces back into a semblance of the original shape of the mirror. And after that had been done, a black pentagram had been painted on the shards; a pentagram with a crude bolt of lightning in the center.

Chapter Five

"Get out of here. *Now.*" Zac's large hand was already closing around Guinevere's arm, crushing the delicate red silk. In this mood one didn't argue with him. Guinevere had seen him like this once or twice, and she knew it wasn't the moment to have a rational discussion.

An instant later she was out in the hallway while Zac meticulously walked through the apartment. By the time he reappeared a few minutes later, she'd had a chance to do some thinking.

"All right," he said quietly, "there's no one here now. Come on back inside." His face was set in hard, cold lines. "Take a good look at that mirror. It's the same kind of pentagram drawing that someone made on Adair's painting, isn't it?"

Guinevere nodded, staring down at the broken mirror. There was something unnaturally menacing about the simple damage, as if the shards of mirror were somehow more threatening than a broken vase would have been, perhaps because of the eerie effect the pieces caused when one looked into them. Guinevere gazed at her shattered reflection and shivered. "It's the same sketch. Someone must have taken the mirror down from the wall and dropped something on it to make it break like this. Then whoever it was drew the pentagram." She lifted her head, her gaze anxious. "Zac, I don't understand."

"Neither do I, but we're going to get some answers tonight." He was already heading toward the door. "This has gone far enough."

"Zac, where are you going?" She didn't like the grimness that enveloped him. In its own way it seemed as threatening as the mirror.

"I'm not going anywhere. *We,* however, are going to have an informative little chat with Mason Adair. His problems seem to have become yours. And that makes them mine."

"But, Zac, it's the middle of the night."

"I don't really give a damn what time it is. Move, Gwen. I want those answers and I want them now."

"I don't think Mason's going to know any more about what's going on than we do," she protested, but she obeyed his summons, hurrying forward as he stepped out into the corridor.

"Believe me, he knows a great deal more than we do."

"How do you know?" she demanded as he herded her quickly back down the stairs and out onto the sidewalk.

"Trust me."

"Uh-huh." Guinevere stifled the remainder of her skepticism. Zac was hurrying her along at a brisk pace. She wished she'd had a moment to change into more comfortable shoes. Trotting along a city sidewalk in three-inch heels made one conscious of the social restraints imposed on females in this society, she reflected. "What if he's not home?"

"For his sake he'd better be home. I'm in no mood to wait around for him."

"Zac, you're acting as if this is all Mason's fault."

"As far as I'm concerned, it is. Whatever part of it he's not responsible for, you are. I told you to stay clear of him and this whole mess, didn't I?"

"You're slipping into one of your unreasonable moods, Zac. When you get like this, you're impossible."

"I'll probably get worse as the evening wears on. All in all, it's been a hell of a night."

She found out how he'd gotten into Adair's apartment building the previous evening. When Zac reached the door now, he slipped a small wire out of his jacket pocket and in less than a minute had the security door open. Zac was good with his hands.

He urged her up the stairs and at the top turned her down the hall toward Mason's closed apartment door. In front of it Zac raised his fist and pounded imperiously.

Embarrassed, Guinevere shot a look at the nearest apartment doors, afraid they would spring open to reveal irate tenants. "Zac, don't do that, you'll cause a scene with the neighbors. Try the door bell."

"Pounding on his door is infinitely more satisfying." He raised his hand and slammed the wooden panel once more. It swung open before Zac could strike it again. Mason stood there dressed in only a pair of jeans. He blinked sleepily.

"What the hell? Oh, it's you, Zac. What are you and Gwen doing here at this time of night?"

"We're here to ask you a few questions." Zac was already pushing his way inside, tugging Guinevere after him.

"Well, sure, but why now?" Mason backed obligingly out of the way, his questioning gaze going from Zac's implacable features to Guinevere's apologetic expression.

"I'm sorry about this, Mason," she said. "But I'm afraid there's been a slight, uh, incident over at my apartment, and Zac felt that perhaps you could shed some light on the situation."

"Shed some light?" Mason looked even more perplexed. "I don't understand."

"Neither do I, and Gwen's polite way of phrasing things isn't helping to clarify the situation. Shut up, Gwen. I'll do the talking."

Guinevere raised her eyes ceilingward in silent exasperation but said nothing.

"All right, Adair," Zac said, "I'll lay this out in words even an artist should be able to follow. Gwen and I got back to her apartment tonight and found that someone had been inside. Whoever it was took great pains to crack a mirror and then draw one of those damn pentagram symbols on the broken pieces. The damage looked a lot like what was done to your painting the other night, and after what happened to you last night, I'm finding tonight's little 'incident' too much of a coincidence. Whatever is going on comes under the heading of weird. You are the only one around who's had some connection with weirdness. I want the whole story, including the rundown on that crazy group of witches you supposedly hung out with a couple of years ago."

Mason glanced helplessly at Guinevere. "Witches?"

"I'm sorry, Mason," she said softly. "I told Zac a little about that crowd you were involved with. I thought he might see some connection between them and what's been happening to you."

"Don't apologize, Gwen. I'm the one who should be sorry. I had no idea anything like this would happen."

"What exactly is happening, Mason?" she asked gently.

He swung away in obvious frustration, starting to pace the floor in front of the arching studio window. Across the way there was a glow through closed mini-blinds, reminding Guinevere that she must have left the lights on earlier in her kitchen. She didn't recall doing so. Perhaps the intruder had switched them on while prowling through her apartment. It gave her chills to think of someone invading her privacy that way.

"I'm sorry," Mason said again, sounding shaken. "I'm really sorry, Gwen."

"Sorry isn't going to get us anywhere." Zac sounded

completely untouched by Mason's obvious distress. "Talk, Adair."

Mason stopped in front of a half finished canvas, shoving his hands dejectedly into his back pockets. He shook his head. "Zac, I honestly don't know what this is all about. That group I was involved with two years ago doesn't exist anymore. At least none of the people who were my friends are still in it."

Guinevere thought back to something Mason had told her on the way back from the art gallery. "You said something about leaving it when some of the members started getting too serious."

Mason nodded. "I did leave it. So did just about everyone else."

"But there were some left in it?" Zac demanded.

Mason hesitated. "Possibly."

"Possibly? Come on, Adair, you can be a little more specific than that. I'm not going to play twenty questions with you. I don't have much patience left this evening. I want to know everything you know and I want to know it now."

Guinevere opened her mouth to urge Zac to lay off but changed her mind when she saw the relentless expression in his eyes. Nothing she could do or say at this point would deflect him. There was no point in trying. Mason looked at his canvas as if studying it in great detail. Slowly he began to explain.

"I'll tell you what I know, Zac, but it isn't much. A couple of years ago some friends of mine got off on this occult kick. It was just a joke, an excuse to roll a few joints and drink a little booze, read some poetry, and, well, party. We were all struggling to make it with our art. Most of us were just barely scraping by, waiting tables or working in bookstores. We were a group with a lot of things in common."

"What did you have in common besides art?" Guinevere asked.

"Oh, the usual. None of our families approved of either our career goals or our life-styles. We were all living at the poverty level and we kind of supported each other emotionally. When times got really tough, we supported each other financially. It was a close-knit group for a while."

"And then some of you started selling your art?" Zac leaned against one high-ceilinged wall, folding his arms across his chest. His penetrating gaze never left Mason.

Mason nodded. "Yeah. Patty started finding a market for her ceramics, and then Walt sold a few pictures. Sylvia got lucky with her prints. Nothing big, but enough to give everyone hope."

"And make a few people envious?" Zac didn't stir from his position against the wall.

"I didn't think so at the time," Mason said slowly. "I honestly didn't think so. We were too close for that."

"Don't feed yourself that line," Zac told him. "Whenever a tight-knit group of struggling nonsuccesses suddenly starts producing a few successes, someone is going to get mad. Believe me. It's human nature."

Mason glared at his painting. "As far as I know, none of the others ever had anything like this happen to them during the past couple of years. I was one of the last of the group to get lucky with my art. Why should someone wait until now to pick on me?"

Zac shrugged. "Maybe because you're getting lucky in such a big way. One of your paintings was hanging in Elizabeth Gallinger's home tonight. Gwen tells me that's the big time, Mason. A real sign of success. Maybe one of your ex-buddies resents one of the group breaking out in such a showy style. Who knows? We'll get to that part later. Go on with your story about this cheerful little party club."

"Well, there isn't much to tell. We got together on Saturday evenings at Ron Sandwick's house."

"Where's that?" Zac interrupted.

"Up on Capitol Hill. One of those old-style places." Mason grimaced. "Run-down neighborhood. Lots of atmosphere."

"Is that why you chose it?"

Mason shook his head. "No. We used it because it was available. Sandwick had inherited it. But he couldn't afford to keep up the payments for long. Not on a starving artist's income. He put it up for sale almost as soon as it was his. But it didn't move very quickly. The real estate market had been flat for ages, and that old place would have been a real millstone around anyone's neck. All the old plumbing and electrical wiring needed repair, not to mention the decaying basement. Sandwick finally unloaded it through a real esate agent about six months ago. An all-cash deal, he said. He took the money and split for the South Seas to play Gauguin. He still owes me fifty bucks," Mason added reflectively.

Zac assimilated that. "Tell me exactly why the group drifted apart."

"A couple of new people joined," Mason said quietly.

"Who brought them into the group?"

"I'm not sure, exactly. I think they were friends of Sandwick, but to tell you the truth it was never really clear. All I knew was that these two started showing up on Saturday nights and they were really into the occult bit. For them it was more than a joke."

Guinevere shot a glance at Zac, who was obviously about to ask another question. She slipped one in instead. "How do you know they were taking it seriously, Mason?"

"Oh, they started insisting on the accuracy of the stupid little rituals we played with when we wanted to pretend we were reaching into the next dimension. They brought in old books that had specific rules for the way things should be done. Until those two came along we just lit a few candles in the basement, poured some wine, and did a little chanting. But they insisted on black candles and chants they got out of one of their nutty books."

"Did anything supernatural ever happen?" Guinevere asked, fascinated.

Mason smiled wryly. "Of course nothing ever happened. How could it? Don't tell me you actually believe in that kind of thing?"

Guinevere shook her head hastily, aware of Zac's derisive glance. "Absolutely not. I just wondered if anything, well, abnormal ever occurred during these ceremonies."

"Valonia and Baldric sometimes claimed they could see into the next dimension and claimed they were 'feeding' on power from it, but it was all a bunch of cow fertilizer."

Zac cocked a brow. "Valonia and Baldric?"

"Those were the two who started demanding the proper rituals."

"Were they artists too?"

Mason paused, considering. "You know, I was never real sure what they did for a living. But I don't think they were part of the Seattle art world, either the low end or the high end. I've never run into them since those Saturday-night gatherings at Sandwick's."

Zac took a small pad of paper out of his pocket and started making notes. "Are they still living in Sandwick's place?"

"No. They never did live there as far as I know. Like I said, Sandwick sold the old house six months ago, anyway. Whoever Valonia and Baldric were, they couldn't have afforded to buy it. They definitely didn't have that kind of money."

"You're sure?"

"Positive. They were one step off the streets. Maybe not even that far. Baldric always wore a huge backpack, and Valonia carried a big satchel. I got the feeling that they lived out of both. They were pretty scruffy and sometimes a little hungry too. The Saturday-night group broke up, and I never saw or heard from those two again."

"But you did keep in touch with the others?" Guinevere asked.

"Oh, sure. To some extent. I know where most of them are. One or two moved down to Southern California. Sandwick left the country. A couple bought a house in the woods down in Oregon as soon as they started selling their stuff. And the other two are here in town. They're doing okay. I was the last of them to start selling."

"The pentagram," Zac said musingly. "Was that part of the Saturday-night rituals?"

"Sometimes," Mason admitted. "Pentagrams are a very common magical symbol. Traditional, even. But the ones our group used in the beginning didn't have that jag of lightning in it. Valonia and Baldric added that little nuance."

"I assume Valonia and Baldric are the only names you knew them by?" Zac asked.

"Yeah, and I'd be willing to bet that they made them up or got them out of one of their damn books on witchcraft. Who ever heard of anyone being named Valonia and Baldric?"

Zac nodded and fell into a remote silence. Guinevere peered at him expectantly. She knew what was happening. He was slipping into one of his private trances during which odd little connections would be made inside his careful, methodical brain. When he came out of the contemplation, he would be aimed in the same way a glacier was aimed down a mountainside and he'd be just as unstoppable. In the meantime Zac might stay in this disengaged mood for a very long time.

"Zac?" she prompted, aware of Mason's curious stare. "Zac? We'd better be going. It's late and Mason's told you everything he knows." She touched his arm. She thought he was at least minimally aware of her.

"The cops," he said distinctly.

Mason looked alarmed, and Guinevere understood instantly. "No," she said. "We can't call the police again, Zac."

"The hell we can't."

"Zac, listen to me, if we call the cops again, news of this weird stuff is going to leak out. We both know that. Some sharp-eyed reporter is going to have a great time with hints of witchcraft surrounding a young new artist who's exploding on the local art scene. Mason's career is just getting launched. This sort of thing could ruin him before he's gotten established. Do you think people like Elizabeth Gallinger will want to be associated with anything that even hints of the occult?"

"Mason is free to do what he wants," Zac said. "It's you I'm worried about."

"Well, let me assure you that any publicity linking me to some occult group isn't going to do me a damn bit of good, either," she reminded him forcefully. "Zac, please, you've got to treat this just as you would any other business case. Your clients call on you precisely because they want to avoid awkward publicity. Think of Mason and me as being clients who want this handled discreetly."

Zac's mouth twitched. "You and Mason can't afford my usual fees."

"Zac!" Guinevere was shocked.

He came away from the wall. "Forget it. A small joke. Stop worrying for now, both of you. I'm not going to call in the cops, but only because I don't think they'd get very far as this point. There just isn't enough here to go on. We need more information before we can turn it over to them. And I don't want Guinevere's name dragged into this mess, Adair."

The younger man nodded. "I understand. I don't particularly want my own name dragged into it. I swear, Zac, I don't have the slightest idea what's going on here. I just can't believe one of my old buddies has gone crazy with envy. And Baldric and Valonia weren't into art, so why should they be envious? I doubt if they would even know I've started selling."

Guinevere recalled something Carla had said. "My sister thought that some of the freeloaders who showed up at the gallery the other night weren't all that happy to see you making it so big. And that Henry Thorpe person sounded as if he might have a back-stabbing sort of nature."

"Forget Thorpe. He had nothing to do with that group," Mason said firmly.

"But he knew about it. He's the one who first mentioned it to me."

"He might have been aware that a few of us hung around together and got up to some weird things, but he was never close to any of the members. He wouldn't have been aware of the pentagram with the bolt of lightning in it, for example."

Zac shook his head. "Maybe. Maybe not. I want both of you to understand something here. My main concern is Gwen. I don't want her business reputation tarnished by having people gossiping about an association with witchcraft. But more importantly, I don't want her physically threatened or hurt. From now on I'll be staying with her at night, either next door or at my place. During the daytime, Mason, I want you to put your window to good use. We'll leave the blinds in Gwen's kitchen window open all the time. If you ever see them closed or if you see anyone moving around inside whom you don't recognize, call me. Call Gwen, too, and tell her not to go into her apartment until I'm around."

Mason nodded. "Got it. I spend a lot of time right here in the studio during the day. I'll keep an eye on things.

Gwen says you investigate security problems for people. Does this mean you're taking me on as a client?"

"I don't seem to have much choice." Zac took Guinevere's arm again and led her toward the door. "Why is it," he complained to her, "that you always manage to get me into these situations?"

"You're not so good on your own," she told him cheerfully, as the door closed behind them. "Just remember what happened to you tonight at Queen Elizabeth's party. Your genes were about to be summoned for royal service."

Zac went a dull red in the dim hall light. "If you had a charitable bone in your body, woman, you wouldn't remind me of that incident. It was one of the worst moments of my entire life. I had no idea that all that talk of biological clocks was leading up to that . . . that proposition she made."

"Poor Zac. Now you know how a woman feels when her boss gives her all sorts of encouragement and support and then expects her to pay him back with a few bouts in bed. You've just been the victim of job harassment."

"I still can't believe it," Zac muttered as they walked down the street to Gwen's apartment.

"If I were you, I'd finish up the Gallinger project very quickly and get your fee. That woman didn't get where she is today by being anything less than tenacious."

"It was probably just a terrible misunderstanding."

"The hell it was," Guinevere retorted spiritedly. "That woman wants a stud, and you're the chosen male."

"Do all women become that . . . that forceful when they decide they have to have a baby?" Zac asked in subdued tones.

"I don't know."

Zac slid an assessing glance at her as he walked beside her up the stairs. "Are you sure, Gwen?"

She heard the genuine concern in his voice and wasn't certain how to interpret it. What was Zac trying to say?

That he might be looking for a woman who was interested in having babies? Someone other than Elizabeth Gallinger? She wished desperately that she knew more about his feelings for her. The desire to be a father might be as sudden and strong in some men as the need to be a mother was in some women. Guinevere felt as if she were walking on eggs. One misstep and she might crush the fragile relationship that existed between herself and Zac.

"I'll let you know if I ever change my mind," she tried to say lightly as she opened her door.

"You do that," he said behind her. "You make sure you do that. I don't want you going hunting the way Elizabeth Gallinger is hunting."

Fortunately the shattered mirror provided a timely distraction. Guinevere walked across the floor and looked at it once again. "What now, Zac?"

He tugged at his tie. "First we pick up the pieces and then we go to bed."

"No, I mean, what happens next in this case?"

"I don't think of this as a *case* exactly," he told her as he unbuttoned the first button of his shirt. "I see it as more in the nature of a damned nuisance."

"But what are we going to do next?"

"I think," Zac said thoughtfully, "that I'll go take a look at that old house on Capitol Hill for starters."

"But Mason said it had been sold six months ago," Guinevere protested impatiently.

"We'll see."

"Now, Zac, don't go all enigmatic and cryptic on me. Tell me why you want to take a look at that old place."

"Simple curiosity. And because it's a starting point. Probably a dead end, but you never know."

Guinevere eyed him thoughtfully, aware of the first faint ripple of excitement she always got when she was involved in one of Zac's more exciting investigations. He claimed he didn't like this kind of thing, and she was inclined to believe him. He was cut out to be a staid, plodding, methodical analyzer of other people's security problems. But occasionally other people's security problems had a way of blowing up into intriguing, sometimes dangerous situations. And Zac coped. Very well.

"When do we go take this look?" Guinevere demanded.

"Don't look so excited. You're not going with me."

"But, Zac—"

"I mean it, Gwen. I'm not taking you along. I have no way of knowing what I'll run into, and whoever clobbered Mason last night might have gotten a good look at you through the window. If there is someone interesting still hanging around that old house, I don't want him to see you. It would only tip him off."

"But you said that going to the old place is probably just a dead end," she reminded him as she scooped up broken bits of mirror and put them in a paper sack.

"I'm not taking any chances. Not where you're involved."

She heard the steel in his voice and reluctantly stopped trying to argue. There were times when you had to go around Zac because you certainly couldn't go through him. "So when are you going to take this look?"

"In a few hours. I'll set the alarm for three."

"Three in the morning? Isn't that a little early?"

Zac shrugged, taking the paper bag from her and putting it carefully into the hall closet instead of into the garbage. "It's a good time to have a look around. Not many people up and about at three in the morning."

Guinevere went toward him, aware of a growing sense of anxiety. "I'd feel better if I went along."

"No, Gwen. Not this time."

She sighed as her arms went around his neck. "Sometimes you can be a very stubborn man."

"We all have some strong points," he agreed philosophically. His hands wrapped around her waist. "Have I thanked you for coming to my rescue tonight at Gallinger's house?"

"I wasn't sure for a while if you wanted to be rescued."

"Believe me, I wanted rescue."

"She's very beautiful and very rich, Zac."

"I want to be loved for myself, not my genes," he said as he began undoing the fastenings of the red silk dress.

Did he mean it? Guinevere asked herself silently as the red dress slipped to the floor. Did he really want to be loved or was it only one of those throwaway remarks people make when they want to lighten a situation? She wished she knew for certain. There was a great deal she did not yet know about Zachariah Justis. Some things she might never know. But he was here tonight, and that would do for now. She lifted her face for his kiss and closed her eyes as she felt the familiar male hunger reach out to enclose her.

Zac felt the soft swell of her breasts against his chest and forgot about biological clocks and embarrassing confrontations with clients. When Guinevere was in his arms, she was all that mattered. The extent of her response to him filled him with a heady satisfaction that wiped out everything else in the vicinity. This was one element of her nature that he could read with certainty. She was the most responsive, the most honest woman he had ever held.

"If you ever want my genes," he told her thickly as he put her down on the bed and came down beside her, "you can have them for free."

"I'll remember that." Her eyes gleamed up at him in the shadows as she took him into her waiting softness.

Three hours and fifteen minutes later Zac awoke with the alertness he felt only when things were getting nasty. He didn't like the feeling, but he had learned to respect it over the years. He was ahead of the alarm clock and reached out carefully to switch it off before it could ring. Five minutes to three.

Quietly he got out of bed, hoping not to wake Guinevere. But as he pulled on his slacks he realized that she was watching him.

"I'll have coffee waiting for you when you get back," she promised.

He grinned in spite of himself. "If you're planning to use that red-and-black monstrosity to make it, you'd better start early." He leaned over her, planting a hand on each side of her on the bedding. Then he kissed her. "See you by five."

Guinevere wanted to say something else, but there wasn't time. He vanished silently through her bedroom door.

Her staid, plodding, methodical Zac was once again on the hunt.

Chapter Six

The house had once been a stately, if rather overwrought, home for a successful businessman during the first part of the century. Now it was what real estate people liked to call a fixer-upper. The streetlight directly in front of the sagging porch was out, but with the fretful moonlight Zac could see that the plump wooden columns that flanked the steps were badly chipped, as if someone had idly carved on them with a pocketknife. The place had once been painted gray, if one could judge by what remained of the old paint. The porch wrapped most of the way around the aging two-story structure, and the weeds in the uncared-for garden were as high as the railing in some places. The screen door appeared to have given up the ghost long ago. It hung lethargically on its hinges. Someone or something had kicked a hole in the bottom part of the screen. No one had bothered to repair it. There was no light in any of the windows.

Zac quietly walked through the backyard of a vacant house next door to what had once been the Sandwick place. He assumed the house was vacant because of the FOR SALE sign in the front yard, but he didn't take any chances. About half the houses in the neighborhood had FOR SALE signs in the front yards. So far he had been lucky enough not to arouse any dogs in the area, and he was hoping to keep it that way.

The neighborhood was one of the streets near Capitol

Hill that had not yet been rehabilitated by the upwardly mobile types who had been moving into the district in droves during the past few years. The Sandwick house was slightly more run-down-looking than its neighbors but not significantly so. Whoever had paid cash for it several months ago had obviously not had a lot left over to effect even minor repairs.

Moving quietly and without the aid of a flashlight, Zac made his way around to the rear of the house Adair and his friends had once used for their occult games. When he reached the back steps, he paused and glanced up at the unlit windows with a certain morose resignation.

This wasn't, Zac decided, the kind of investigation he thought appropriate to the newly emerging image of Free Enterprise Security, Inc. It was his firm's mission to cater to the security needs of sophisticated businesses. He was supposed to be a consultant, for God's sake. One who charged very large fees in return for reports bound in genuine, simulated leather binders. This business of sneaking through decaying neighborhoods to spy on an old house that once might or might not have been used for witchcraft definitely came under the heading of tacky. Very low-class. And it was all Guinevere's fault.

He thought of Guinevere as he had left her over half an hour ago. She had been lying in the tousled bed, her dark hair tumbling around her bare shoulders, eyes wide and a little worried in the shadows. Zac admitted to himself that he rather liked it when she became anxious on his behalf. He couldn't remember anyone else in recent history who had ever really worried about him. Already he was looking forward to the coffee and concern that would be waiting for him when he returned from this sortie into the wilds of Capitol Hill. A man could get used to the idea of someone waiting for him.

No use putting off the inevitable. The sooner he was finished here, the sooner he could collect both the coffee and Guinevere. Silently Zac started up the back steps of the house. At the rear door he paused and let the tiny sounds and nuances of the night infiltrate his heightened sense of awareness.

Zac could usually tell when a place was occupied. There was a sense of presence about a room or a house or a building that made itself felt. It wasn't anything concrete, just a kind of instinctive awareness. There had been times in the past when that kind of awareness had kept him alive. There had also been occasions when it had let him down at awkward moments. He hoped this wasn't going to be one of those moments. Zac didn't fool himself. He wasn't psychic; he simply had fairly well developed survival instincts. But they weren't infallible.

Still, there was nothing to indicate that anyone was at home here tonight. Zac slipped into the deeper shadows of the porch and examined the lock on the back door. Piece of cake. He pulled the small twist of metal out of his pocket and, a moment later, let himself into what proved to be the kitchen.

As he eased the door shut behind him he stood still for another few seconds, trying to pick up any new vibrations that might indicate the presence of another person.

The house was silent. Perhaps too silent. Zac frowned thoughtfully and walked through the kitchen. The refrigerator was turned off, and there were no dishes standing in the chipped sink. He was about to make his way into the next room when he saw the Styrofoam hamburger containers in a paper sack by the stove. Someone had made a recent foray to a fast-food restaurant and brought the results back here to eat.

Zac considered the possibilities. A transient might be using the place to bed down at night. A workman might have been commissioned to do some repairs and had brought a fast-food lunch with him. Neighborhood kids might have been using the old house as a hangout. There were a variety of potential answers to the questions raised by the burger container. Zac didn't like most of them.

The floor beneath his feet was hardwood, and it had survived in better condition than most of the rest of the house. Zac was cautious as he moved into the breakfast room, but there were no squeaks or groans.

There were a few pieces of furniture in the breakfast room and also in the parlor he found on the other side. None of them were in decent condition. No one had even bothered to cover the few chairs, tables, and the sofa. Zac could smell the damp, dusty odor emitted by disintegrating fabric in every room. The only reason he could see at all was because the drapes were in such tatters that the vague streetlight could filter in through the large windows.

He found the staircase in the front hall. It was broad, heavily banistered, and still sturdy. The shadows were thicker on the second floor because the windows were smaller and allowed less moonlight and light from the street to enter. There was no more evidence of recent habitation, but Zac found himself using more caution than should have been necessary under the circumstances. It was a good thing he'd had the sense to make Guinevere stay behind. She would have been running around, exploring and investigating like an eager puppy. Guinevere tended to be both impulsive and a little reckless, Zac thought with indulgent disapproval. He wondered if he was going to spend the rest of his life getting himself dragged into a series of adventures such as this one.

The odd part was that in the beginning, when he had first contacted her, he'd entertained a few notions of using Guinevere on certain kinds of cases. Her temporary-help business provided an ideal cover for planting an observer in almost any sort of firm. Everyone needed secretaries and clerks, and no one paid much attention to them, not even when they were temporary replacements. But lately, Zac noted wryly, he seemed to be the one getting involved in Guinevere's adventures, rather than vice versa.

The upper floor was as empty as the first. There was an old, tilted bed in one room with a lumpy, stained mattress. Zac didn't get the feeling it had been used in the past several years. If some transient was using the house at night, he wasn't sleeping in the bedrooms.

Getting up at three this morning had probably been a waste of time and energy. He could just as easily have stayed in bed with Guinevere and learned as much. Zac headed back downstairs, still moving cautiously.

In the kitchen he glanced around once more and idly opened a few cupboard doors. Most of the shelves were empty, although there were a couple of grungy mugs in one cupboard.

He was hunting for the broom closet when he opened the door that revealed a flight of stairs down to a basement. The door had a key-activated bolt on it, but no one had locked it that night. Perhaps not for a long time.

Zac paused on the threshold and tried to analyze what it was that seemed different about the dank odor wafting up from the dark pit at the bottom of the steps. He couldn't see a thing past the first two or three treads.

For the first time he removed the small, pencil-slim flashlight from the pocket of his windbreaker. Closing the basement door behind him so that light wouldn't escape back into the kitchen, he flicked on the narrow beam.

At first he could see nothing but a few more steps. The utter darkness of the basement seemed to crowd in on the small band of light as if trying to devour it. For the first time since he had entered the house Zac felt a tiny frisson of awareness. Grimly he shook it off. He was letting his imagination take over. Not a common state of affairs. Once again he thanked his lucky stars he'd held the line with Gwen and refused to let her accompany him. *Her* imagination would be having a field day down here.

Slowly he started down the steps. The flashlight fought back bravely against the overpowering darkness, and Zac followed in its wake. It seemed a long way down to the concrete floor, but eventually he reached the last step. His imagination was not settling down, he noticed.

Methodically he turned to the right at the bottom of the steps, prowling along one wall. He didn't see the heavy black drapes until he nearly blundered into them. One moment he was feeling his way along a cold, damp surface, and the next his hand tangled with thick velvet cascading from the low ceiling all the way to the floor. Startled, Zac stopped and shone the light along the entire surface of the black drapes.

As far as he could tell, there was nothing but basement wall behind the wide expanse of fabric. Certainly there was no window to be shielded. It didn't take much investigative talent to realize that, unlike the torn and rotting fabric on the windows upstairs, these drapes were in good condition.

Zac edged back, playing the light on the fabric as he studied it. He had to move back quite a ways to see the full extent of the velvet wall coverings. The velvet hung in heavy folds along most of one entire wall. Who the hell would drape a basement in black velvet?

Zac didn't like the possible answers to his questions. Perhaps this was a leftover from the days when Adair and his friends had held their little parties here. The new owners of the house might not have bothered to take down the drapes. They certainly hadn't bothered to make any repairs or modifications. Perhaps they hadn't even seen their new acquisition. Zac made a note to find out who the legal owner was as soon as the appropriate county offices opened for business that day. The information probably wouldn't do him any good, but Zac liked to have all the loose ends accounted for.

He took another step backward, marveling over the extent of what must have been very expensive, if very ugly, drapery, and promptly collided with a cold, unyielding surface. Zac swung around and let the flashlight beam run along the edge of a long, high table.

It wasn't, Zac decided grimly, exactly a Formica-topped dining room table. This monstrosity was at least six feet long and appeared to be made out of some sort of black stone. It was supported by three squat columns that had clawed feet.

The uneasy flicker of awareness sizzled lightly over his nerve endings once more. This time Zac decided not to ignore it. He switched off the flashlight in the same instant that he felt the small disturbance in the air behind him. Zac threw himself to one side, but the heavy metal object that had been descending toward his head didn't miss him entirely. It glanced along the side of his skull and landed with numbing force on his left shoulder.

Zac spun around, his body automatically following the direction of the blow in an effort to lessen the impact. There was a stifled grunt as his right fist landed in the center of a man's chest. It was pure luck as far as Zac was concerned. The impetus of the man's rush had carried him straight into Zac's instinctively raised hand.

The thing about luck was that it didn't do you any good unless you took advantage of it. With no feeling at all in his left shoulder Zac had to rely entirely on his right arm. In the utter darkness he could see nothing of his attacker, but the man's heavy, scrabbling body was easy enough to locate. It was all over Zac.

Whoever he was, he still had the metal object he'd used a few seconds earlier. Zac struggled to land a decent, chopping blow before the other man could swing again. There was another grunt as Zac found a solid, if slightly soft, target in the stomach region. He brought his knee up, hoping for a more vulnerable area.

But the attacker was staggering backward, blundering into the table. Zac's maneuver landed slightly off target.

There was a vicious curse as the other man hit the stone and Zac followed the direction of the sound. He aimed another chopping blow at what should have been the neck region and connected with what must have been a shoulder. Then a wild, swinging kick from a booted foot caught Zac on the thigh, sending him staggering against the curtained wall.

When his left shoulder struck the wall, Zac realized that the numbing effect of the blow was wearing off. Streaks of agony laced through his arm and shoulder, making him suck in his breath and struggle to keep his senses from reeling into a darkness that was greater than that of the basement.

The shock of the pain drove him to his knees. Through the daze he could hear frantic shuffling sounds from his attacker and braced himself for another assault. If the man rushed him, Zac decided the only thing he could do was hit the floor and hope the other guy crashed into the wall.

But the other basement denizen wasn't planning any more heroic attacks. The shuffling sounds sorted themselves out into footsteps, and a few seconds later Zac heard the man on the stairs. Apparently whoever it was knew his way around the basement far better than Zac. The door at the top of the stairs opened briefly, revealing a rectangle of lighter shadow, and then it slammed shut again. There was no sound of a key in the lock. Perhaps the escaping man didn't have the key, or maybe he just didn't want to take the extra time it would take to lock the door to the basement.

Zac struggled awkwardly to his feet, listening for the sounds that would tell him whether his assailant was escaping or merely going for bigger and better weapons. With a small sense of relief Zac heard the back door slamming shut. It was a very distant echo. The heavy wooden flooring upstairs covered almost all the noise.

His senses swam as Zac managed to straighten into a

more or less standing position. Gingerly he touched his left shoulder with his right hand and winced. But as far as he could tell, nothing was broken. One had to be thankful for small mercies in this sort of situation.

He found the flashlight when he accidentally kicked it with his foot. The frail beam shone listlessly across the dusty basement floor. Bending down, Zac retrieved it and swung it around in an arc. Light fell on the object that had been used to nearly brain him. It was a black metal candlestick, heavy and tall, almost as good as a length of pipe for cracking skulls. Zac left it where it was. All he wanted now was to get out of the basement before whoever he had tangled with returned with assistance. This sort of thing could be potentially embarrassing to an upwardly mobile executive in the security business.

He was starting up the steps when the flashlight beam skimmed along the surface of a long object propped against one side of the staircase. Pausing, Zac ran the beam along the surface and realized that he was looking at a framed painting. A framed Mason Adair painting. There could be no mistaking the brilliant light and clear, vibrant colors. Even here, in a pitch-dark basement, illuminated only by a flashlight, the effect of Adair's work made itself felt. Maybe the guy really had some talent, Zac admitted reluctantly to himself.

Tentatively Zac leaned over the wooden stair rail and tried to lift the framed canvas. It was heavier than he'd expected. There was no question that it would take two hands, and just then Zac didn't have two working hands available. Regretfully he left the canvas where it was and finished the trek up the steps.

The kitchen seemed almost flooded with light compared to the oppressive darkness of the basement. Zac stood blinking in the shadows for a few seconds, letting his eyes adjust as he switched off the flashlight. Then he let himself out the back door.

It seemed a long way back to where he'd parked the Buick. He couldn't risk the sidewalks, so he stuck to backyards and gardens. He briefly noted one particularly thriving crop of an agricultural product generally characterized as an illegal substance. He finally emerged on the street where he'd left the car. It was still there, complete with hubcaps. No one went out of his way to steal three-year-old Buick hubcaps.

He had some movement back in his left arm but no real strength. Using his right hand for everything, Zac fished the car keys out of his pocket and got the reliable engine started. A moment later he was driving sedately out of the area, keeping his headlights off for a couple of blocks until he was sure he wouldn't be observed by anyone who might feel obliged to notice a strange vehicle in the neighborhood and report it. Not that the neighborhood was likely to have a block-watch program. This wasn't the sort of district where people went out of their way to keep an eye on strangers, but there was no point in taking any more chances. Life had been adventurous enough tonight.

Guinevere was pacing the floor at four-thirty when she heard Zac's key in the lock. With a strangled little cry of relief she raced forward, throwing herself into his arms as he opened the door.

"For God's sake, don't do that," Zac hissed painfully as her arms closed tightly around him.

Startled at the distinct lack of welcome in his greeting, Guinevere drew back and eyed him anxiously. "What's wrong?"

"A great deal. My left arm feels as if it may fall off at any moment." He stepped into the room and shut the door behind him.

"Your arm! Zac, what happened? Are you all right?"

"I think I'm going to survive, but I can tell you, Gwen, that this little investigation you've sicced me onto isn't the type of thing I had in mind when I incorporated in the State of Washington. Did you get the coffee made?"

"It's ready. I've been worried, Zac. What on earth happened to your arm? Did you fall?"

"Some joker got me with a candlestick. I'll take a few aspirin with the coffee, if you don't mind."

Guinevere stared at him, appalled. The grimly etched lines around his mouth told their own story, as did the careful way Zac was cradling his left arm. "Maybe we should get you to a doctor."

"No."

"But, Zac . . ."

He gave her a disgusted glance. "Nothing's broken. I'll be all right eventually, although I may not be my usual athletic self in bed for a while."

"This is not the time for sexual humor, Zachariah Justis. Come into the kitchen and sit down. I'll get your coffee and aspirin. Then I want to take a look at that shoulder."

"You can look but don't touch. It's going to be a while before I let anyone touch it. Christ. If I weren't such a macho type, I'd admit that it hurts like hell."

"Oh, Zac . . ."

"I love it when you go all dithering and feminine on me."

"I am not dithering." She urged him into a chair and poured coffee.

"When did you put the coffee on?" he asked, accepting the mug. "The minute I left?"

"Forget the nasty comments on my coffee machine and tell me what happened."

"First the aspirin."

Guinevere hurried into the bathroom and returned a few seconds later with a bottle of tablets. "Here you are. Zac, really, I think you should take off your jacket and shirt and let me see that shoulder."

"Getting out of this jacket right now would put an end to my macho facade. Give me a little time, okay?"

"All right, but I'm worried, Zac."

"So am I. But not about my shoulder."

"Zac, tell me what went on in that house tonight." Guinevere shook her head mournfully. "I knew I should have gone with you."

"Oh, you'd have had a field day. The place would have inspired your imagination." Gratefully he sipped the hot brew.

"Is it haunted?" she demanded.

"If it is, the ghosts aren't the ones causing the problems. The guy who got me with the candlestick was very much alive."

In succinct, unadorned sentences Zac gave her a quick rundown on what had happened in the old Sandwick house, concluding with the discovery of the Mason Adair painting.

"Someone is storing a Mason Adair painting in that awful basement? But why? And what's with the altar and the black velvet drapes?" Guinevere wondered aloud.

"An altar." Zac thought about the stone table. "Yeah, that's a good way to describe it. A black altar."

Guinevere shuddered. "Your description alone is enough to give me the creeps. It must have been horrible going through that basement. Zac, you could have been killed."

"I'm not sure the guy was out to kill me. I think I surprised him and he struck out with the first thing he could find, namely a candlestick. Could have been a transient, someone bedding down illegally in an empty house. I was probably as big a surprise to him as he was to me."

"But you said the black drapes looked in good condition?"

"They were a lot newer than the rest of the furnishings upstairs."

Guinevere chewed on her lower lip, thinking. "Was there a lot of dust on that altar?"

"Good point." Zac closed his eyes, trying to recapture the image of the black stone. "No."

"So someone's taking care of the basement while the rest of the house rots away? Zac, it doesn't make any sense."

"Maybe it will when we find out who bought the place from Sandwick." Zac glanced at the kitchen clock. "In a few more hours I'll go down to the county courthouse and take a look at the land records."

"What about the painting?"

"Describe it to Adair and see if he can remember whether he sold it or gave it to anyone."

Guinevere nodded. "Maybe Theresa, the gallery owner, will know if it was one she sold. Mason hasn't sold too many pictures yet. It shouldn't be hard to figure out who bought a particular one. What did it look like?"

Zac gazed into the depths of his coffee, remembering. "Lots of turquoise and purple. A water scene with lots of glare on the surface of the sea. But the effect was reversed, as if you were under the water looking up at the sun, if you know what I mean."

"Um. I recall that one from the night of Mason's show although I can't remember the title. Why don't I contact both of them and see what I can find out while you check the land records?"

"I knew it," Zac said ruefully.

"Knew what?"

"You're taking charge already. I go out and do the dirty work and then you get to do the executive stuff. It always happens like this."

Guinevere leaned forward, her chin resting on her propped hands. Her eyes were light with warm amusement. "You know what they say about brains and brawn. Besides, it was your idea to do the dirty work alone. I offered to come along and help."

"So you did."

Her amusement disappeared. "Zac, what do you think is going on? None of this makes any sense."

"I'm aware of that. At the moment your guess is as good as mine."

"I keep thinking about the possibility of professional jealousy," Guinevere said slowly. "This all seems a little bizarre for that."

"We live in a bizarre world. People have been known to do ruthless things in the name of professional jealousy. But it's this connection with that occult group that's got me nervous, Gwen. I don't like it. Give me a nice, clean, financially motivated thief or swindler every time. I can understand financial motivation."

Guinevere watched his hand go probingly to his left shoulder. "I'm worried about that shoulder, Zac."

He smiled cryptically. "I like it when you're worried about me."

"Zac, I'm serious."

"So am I."

Mason Adair recognized the description of the painting immediately. He listened as Guinevere stood in his studio later that morning and told him what Zac had seen in the basement of the old house. Slowly he walked to the window and stood looking down onto the street.

"Glare," he said.

"I beg your pardon?" Guinevere countered.

"The name of the picture is *Glare.* It's supposed to be hanging in the Midnight Light gallery. As far as I know, Theresa hasn't sold it."

"Then I think," Guinevere announced firmly, "that we'd better contact Theresa."

"I'll call her now." Mason picked up the phone. Theresa came on the line at once, and even from across the room Guinevere could hear the agitation in the woman's voice.

When Mason finished talking and replaced the receiver, Guinevere was already half prepared for the answer.

"Stolen?" she asked softly.

Mason nodded. "Sometime late yesterday or early last night, Theresa thinks. She was waiting until her assistant got in this morning to make sure it hadn't been sold, but the assistant just arrived and swears it was hanging on the wall until at least four o'clock yesterday."

"Could somebody have just walked out with it?" Guinevere asked. "Or was there some sign of forced entry?"

"No evidence of anyone having tried to break into the gallery. And, yes, someone could have walked out with it. It happens. Security isn't exactly tight around most of the Pioneer Square galleries. There have been a few instances of paintings having disappeared during working hours. Theresa was going to report the theft to the cops. I told her to wait."

"I heard you. Zac's going to find this interesting."

But Zac had news of his own by the time Guinevere called him and told him what she'd learned.

"The house was bought for fifty-five thousand in cash by a Barry Hodges. All the taxes are being kept up-to-date." Zac glanced at his notes as he spoke into the phone. "I talked to some real estate people who checked their multiple listings. They say the house isn't for sale, and no one's got it on the market to rent. The agent who handled the deal said it was a very quick sale, with no real negotiation. Sandwick wanted the money and took the first offer he got."

"Does the agent remember this Barry Hodges?" Guinevere asked.

"She remembers that he didn't look like the type who could come up with fifty-five thousand in cash. I gather he was kind of scruffy, long-haired, and overweight. Said he wanted a fixer-upper and had already picked out the Sandwick place. But so far he hasn't done any fixing. The agent hasn't seen him since he signed the last of the papers."

"How did you get all that information out of her?" Guinevere demanded.

"Innate charm."

"The same sort of charm you seen to have been using lately on Elizabeth Gallinger?" Guinevere kept her tone light, but Zac's lack of response on the other end of the line told her that he didn't appreciate the joke. She rushed to fill the unpleasant silence, wishing she'd kept her mouth shut. "Theresa says the painting probably disappeared late yesterday afternoon, by the way. Mason asked her not to report it to the police."

"That figures. Mason's definitely running scared about jeopardizing his newfound fame and fortune, isn't he?"

"Wouldn't you be, in his shoes? Painting is his business, the same way security work is yours and mine is providing temporary help. He's just as concerned about protecting his image and reputation as any businessman, Zac. Just think of him as a *client.* You're always helping your clients avoid embarrassing publicity."

"Gwen, let's get this straight, once and for all. I am not wasting my time in dark basements for the sake of an artist who might one day be rich but who presently couldn't possibly afford me."

"I know, Zac. You're doing this for me. And I want you to know I really do appreciate it," Guinevere assured him earnestly.

"Good. Because when this is all over, I intend to collect my fee one way or the other. Now, back to business. I think it's time you and I played house."

Guinevere nearly fell out of her office chair. "What?" she got out weakly.

"I may have misstated that. We're going to pretend we're looking for a house."

"To buy?"

"Uh-huh. A fixer-upper in the same neighborhood where the Sandwick house is located. Or maybe I should start calling it the Barry Hodges house. I want an excuse to talk to the neighbors, and people always seem to talk a lot more freely to you than they do to me."

"My innate charm," Guinevere explained loftily.

Chapter Seven

It *was* partly Gwen's charm that people usually responded to so easily, Zac thought as he parked the Buick a block down the street from the Sandwick house. But it was more than that. She had a curiously empathic ability that he knew he lacked completely. It was the empathy that really broke down the barriers, even those of strangers. People would talk freely to Guinevere when they wouldn't have given him the time of day. He glanced at her appraisingly as they started up the weed-strewn sidewalk.

"I'm seeing a whole new you," Zac remarked, eyeing the tight curve of her derriere in her faded blue jeans. With the jeans she wore a sporty plaid shirt. "Do you realize how different you look this afternoon?"

"This is my country-western look," Guinevere explained, patting her hair, which was worn long and anchored with a clip. "From what you told me about the neighborhood I didn't think I should show up here in my new suit from Nordstrom's. We're supposed to be a struggling young couple trying to buy a first house, right?"

"We *are* a struggling young couple," Zac told her.

"Not so young, I'm afraid."

Zac shot her another sidelong glance. "Is that worrying you?"

"Everyone worries about getting older."

"Yeah, but women have to worry about that biological clock thing on top of everything else."

Guinevere wished she'd kept her mouth shut. "Back to clocks, are we? What is it with you lately, Zac? I thought you'd learned your lesson the hard way last night at Elizabeth Gallinger's house."

"Forget it. Now listen to me. I don't want you saying too much or letting anyone know we might be anything other than just prospective home buyers checking out the neighborhood. Act like we're engaged."

Guinevere considered that. "First marriage or second?"

"For Pete's sake, Gwen, you don't have to get that detailed about the story."

"This is my first time as an undercover agent. I want to be a success."

Zac muttered something she didn't quite catch and then said firmly, "We'll try that lady in her garden across the street."

Guinevere glanced around at the seedy front lawn of the house they were passing. "I think there are a couple of people working in the backyard of this place. Why not start here?"

"I don't think those two will be too chatty."

"Why not?"

Zac took her arm to help her across the quiet street. "I went through their backyard last night. They've got a very healthy crop of marijuana growing back there."

"No kidding? You don't think they'll want to share some gardening tips?" Guinevere grinned up at him. "What on earth were you doing wandering around their backyard?"

"I was hoping I'd be less conspicuous that way. People walking through quiet neighborhoods such as this at three in the morning tend to cause comment."

"Last night must have been exciting for you," Guinevere observed.

"Oh, it was."

They ambled along the sidewalk with a deliberately casual air, talking in low tones. When they reached the house Zac had selected, a fat gray cat strode into their path, meowing authoritatively. Guinevere went down on her haunches and held out her hand. The cat regarded it arrogantly for a few seconds and then trotted forward to investigate.

"Hope you don't mind cats," said a surprisingly husky, female voice. "Old Jumper there is my guard cat." The comment was followed by a hoarse chuckle that ended up in a smoker's cough.

Zac smiled blandly at the small elderly woman on the other side of the sagging picket fence. "My fiancée loves animals. When we get a house of our own, she's hoping to get a couple of cats."

Guinevere glanced up, smiling, as she stroked Jumper's ears. "How do you do? I'm Guinevere Jones. This is my, uh, fiancé, Zac Justis. We were having a look around the neighborhood. Our real estate agent said there were a couple of places for sale here that might be in our price range."

"Abby Kettering," the older woman offered cheerfully enough as she withdrew a pack of unfiltered cigarettes from the pocket of her gardening apron. She lit one and inhaled vigorously. Abby Kettering was probably close to eighty, her thin hair a wispy white cloud around heavily lined features. Sharp brown eyes shone like buttons in her face. She let out the smoky breath in a long sigh of satisfaction and regarded the tip of her cigarette. "Doctor says I shoulda quit these things forty years ago. I told him there wasn't much point in quitting now. Aren't that many fun things to do when you get to be my age. House hunting, huh?"

Guinevere nodded, straightening. "That's right. Something affordable. A place we could fix up on our own as the money comes in. Prices here in Seattle are pretty steep, we've found. You like this neighborhood?"

Abby gazed speculatively up and down the run-down block. "Let's just say I own this place free and clear. That puts a rosy glow on the whole neighborhood as far as I'm concerned."

Guinevere laughed. "I understand completely."

"Who knows?" Abby went on philosophically, inhaling on her cigarette, "maybe one of these days we'll get selected for one of those big rehabilitation grants. Or maybe some developer will come in and want to buy up the whole block for a hotel or something." She leaned against the fence, which gave a little beneath her weight. "This used to be a pretty nice area, you know," she went on wistfully. "Back when my husband was alive, all these houses were full of families. People took care of their gardens. Didn't let 'em run to pot the way that bunch down the street has." She broke out in another hoarse chuckle. "Pot. Get it? They got a bunch of marijuana growing in the backyard."

"Good grief," said Zac, looking appropriately appalled.

"Stingy as all get-out too," Abby continued. "Not at all neighborly. I asked 'em for a little bit just for my own personal use and they wouldn't give me a single leaf. And after all the zucchini bread I've taken over to 'em." She shook her head. "Young people these days. They just don't understand the meaning of neighborliness."

"I suppose you're right," Guinevere agreed sadly.

Abby opened the creaky gate. "Long as you're just casing the area, why don't you come out back for a glass of iced tea? Wouldn't want you to get too bad an impression of the folks around here."

"That's very kind of you, Mrs. Kettering," Guinevere said as Zac immediately propelled her through the gate.

"Call me Abby." Abby Kettering led the way around to the backyard and seated Zac and Guinevere in an old porch swing while she went into the kitchen to pour three glasses of iced tea. When she reappeared a few minutes later, she smiled. "So you two are gonna get married, huh?"

"That's right," Zac said, lightly touching Guinevere's hand.

"Neither one of you looks like you're just outta high school. This gonna be a first or second marriage?"

"First," said Zac.

"Second," said Guinevere simultaneously.

Abby wrinkled her nose. "You ain't sure?"

"Well," said Guinevere, lowering her eyes demurely, "it's my first. Zac's second." She ignored Zac's irritated movement beside her.

"Gotcha." Abby leaned back in her lawn chair, nodding to herself. "You got some pretty heavy-duty alimony and child support to pay from that first marriage, Zac?"

"Uh . . ."

Guinevere moved to cover Zac's floundering response. "It's one of the reasons we have to find an inexpensive house, Abby. What with all the money that has to go to Zac's ex-wife and four kids, there just isn't a lot left over at the end of the month." There was a choking sound from Zac that turned into a cough. "We've spotted a couple of places on this street that might do for us. There's one two doors down that has a for-sale sign in front of it."

Abby nodded complacently. "The Comstock place. Comstocks moved out a few months ago when they split up. Put the house on the market but it's been damn tough to sell houses in this area for the past few years. They're probably getting desperate. You might get a real good deal on it."

"Actually, I like the one next to it better," Guinevere said musingly. "The old two-story place with the wrap-around porch? I just love those huge, old-fashioned porches."

Abby frowned, thinking. "Oh, I expect you mean the Sandwick place. It was for sale for a long time, but that

Sandwick boy finally found a buyer a few months ago. Far as I know, it ain't for sale now."

"Is that right?" Zac frowned. "But there doesn't appear to be anyone living there. We just assumed it was up for sale. Are you sure it was sold a few months ago?"

"Sure as hell. I talked to the guy who was scouting it out for some big-time investor back East. He was just like you two. Asked a lot of questions about the area. Said the hot shot he represented wanted to invest in some low-income fixer-uppers out here in Seattle, but he was a little uncertain about the neighborhood. I told him I thought the place had real potential 'cause we're so close to Capitol Hill, and Lord knows Capitol Hill has gotten downright trendy in the past few years. One of these days we might get trendy too."

Zac leaned forward to set down his tea glass, his movements deliberate. "So this investor's representative went ahead and bought the Sandwick place?"

Abby shrugged. "I guess so. Next thing I knew, the for-sale sign was down."

"He certainly hasn't put any work into the place," Guinevere said disapprovingly. "It's quite run-down."

"Maybe he's just sitting on it until the market picks up," Zac suggested.

Abby lit another cigarette. "Don't know about that. Once in a while I've seen a couple of rough types hanging around the place. Usually late at night. Sometimes these days I don't sleep too good, you know? Ever since my Hank died . . . Well, anyhow, I think I've seen a man and a woman comin' and goin' from there. Sometimes others. Thought at first they might be new tenants. But they just come and go occasionally, mostly at night. Don't appear to live there. Maybe just some street people who've found a vacant house to sleep in when the weather's bad." Abby exhaled a ring of smoke. "Street people. Funny how words change, ain't it? I can remember when we used to call that type bums."

Guinevere summoned up a startled expression. "Bums? There are bums staying in the Sandwick house?"

"They're not so bad," Abby told her reassuringly. "Leastways they're quiet. Not like that rowdy group that used to hold parties there back when the Sandwick boy owned the place. Bunch of beatnik types."

Zac blinked. "Beatniks?"

Abby waved the hand holding the cigarette. "Don't know what they call 'em now. You know, artsy types. Think they're all red-hot painters who are gonna set the world on fire someday. They used to show up over there on Saturday nights and have themselves a good time. Never invited me. Anyways, they're all gone now. They used to be there on a regular basis, but then they stopped holding those wild parties, and next thing I knew, that guy from back East was buying the place for his investor friend. That Sandwick boy owes me something, although he doesn't know it."

"How's that?" Zac asked.

"Well," Abby confided, "if it hadn't been for me talkin' up the potential of the neighborhood, so to speak, I'm not sure that representative feller would have recommended that his pal buy the place. The rep had heard all sorts of rumors about weird things happening over there at the Sandwick place. Asked me a lot of questions about 'em. I reassured him."

"Is that right?" Guinevere tried to look vaguely alarmed. "What sort of weird things, Abby? The place isn't haunted or anything, is it?"

"Good Lord, no!" Abby's laughter dissolved into another wave of coughing. When she recovered, she took a long swallow of tea and shook her head. "No ghosts as far as I know. Seems like that representative guy had heard the parties goin' on were connected with some spooky occult-type stuff. I told him that was most likely a load of nonsense. Just a bunch of young folks having fun. So what if they played a few games? It wasn't anything serious."

"Were they playing occult games there, Abby?" Zac asked with deep concern.

Abby lifted one thin shoulder. "Maybe. A time or two I'd look out late at night and see all the lights go off. Then the house would stay dark for a long time. Sometimes I could see some lights flickering. Maybe candles. But that was the extent of it. Who knows what was going on? My guess is that they were all sitting happily in the parlor getting rocked out of their tiny little minds."

Guinevere frowned. "Rocked?"

"Stoned. Whatever. I forget the word they use. All I know is the young folks get to have all the fun these days." Abby sighed. "Then again, maybe it was always that way. So. When you two gettin' married?"

"We haven't set the date," Zac said clearly, crushing Guinevere's hand as she opened her mouth to respond. "It sort of depends."

"On what?" Abby demanded. "On whether or not Gwen here is pregnant?"

Guinevere choked on her iced tea. Zac pounded her obligingly on the back until she recovered. "Strange you should mention the subject of babies, Abby," Zac went on as he assisted Guinevere. "Gwen and I have been discussing the matter a lot lately."

"If you're gonna have 'em," Abby advised Guinevere, "better start soon. Got to have babies while you're young. How old are you, anyway? Look like you're hoverin' around thirty."

"As a matter of fact, I am," Guinevere admitted, glaring at an innocent-looking Zac. "But it's Zac I'm worried about. He's getting very close to forty, you see."

Abby grinned. "Don't you worry too much about him slowin' down just 'cause he's gettin' near forty. It's not necessarily true that men are over the hill after forty. Lots of 'em keep goin' strong. Take my husband, for instance—"

"Uh, maybe we'd better be on our way," Zac said, interrupting his hostess as gently as possible. "Gwen and I still have a lot to do today. There are a couple of other neighborhoods we're supposed to check out before we make a decision on a house. We certainly do appreciate your advice, Abby. Maybe we'll be neighbors someday." He was urging Guinevere out of the backyard. "Thanks for the iced tea."

"Anytime," Abby called after them. "Anytime at all. Maybe next time you drop in I'll have some of my neighbor's pot to offer you. I'm thinking of offering them something more interesting than zucchini bread by way of a trade. Got some really beautiful beefsteak tomatoes coming along back here. They might go for 'em."

"Good luck, Abby," Guinevere called back. Then she found herself out on the sidewalk in front of the house. Plaintively she looked up at Zac, whose face was set in frozen lines. "What's the rush? The conversation was just getting interesting."

"We got all the useful information we were likely to get."

"Concerning the Sandwick house, maybe, but what about all those pearls of wisdom she was giving me about aging males?"

"Anything you want to know about aging males, you ask me. I'm becoming an authority. I seem to be aging rapidly around you. Ex-wife and four kids. Jesus, Gwen, your sense of humor is weird, you know that?"

"Probably the company I keep. Where to now?"

"Back to the office. Believe it or not, I do have other projects besides this one that require my attention. *Paying* projects."

"Aha. The Gallinger analysis."

"I want to get that final report in and collect my fee." Zac opened the Buick door for her.

"You're certainly in a hurry to wind that business up," Guinevere noted sweetly.

Zac shot her a quelling look as he guided the Buick away from the curb. "When I've finished with the report, I want to have another talk with Adair. Set up a time this evening, will you?"

"Sure. What do you think that 'investor's representative' business is all about? Who do you think it was who asked Abby about the Sandwick house parties?"

"I don't know, but it sure doesn't sound like the same guy who bought the house through the real estate agent. The agent said the client was scruffy and didn't look like he possibly could have put fifty-five grand together. The agent's client sounds more like one of the 'street people' Abby thought might be staying in the place from time to time. I'm hoping Mason might have some more information. Maybe he knows more than he realizes. Give me a call this afternoon after you've set up a time to meet with him."

"You'll be in your office?"

"Either there or over at Gallinger's."

"Keep an eye on your genes."

"I appreciate your concern."

Carla was busy handling a client call when Guinevere returned to the office that afternoon. She had a terrific telephone voice, Guinevere thought as she listened to her sister promise a temporary secretary to one of Camelot Services' better clients. Maybe she should think twice about pushing Carla out on her own. There were times when it was extremely convenient to leave the office in good hands.

"Find out anything useful?" Carla asked expectantly as she hung up the phone.

"Maybe. Zac's not sure. One of the neighbors said she thought the Sandwick house had been sold to a big-time East Coast investor. Yet the real estate agent says the buyer was a grungy, long-haired local. Zac wants to talk to Mason again. I'm supposed to set up an appointment for all of us this evening."

"I'll do it," Carla said, reaching for the phone immediately.

Guinevere raised one brow but said nothing. Her sister's eagerness to talk to Mason Adair was almost amusing.

"Mason? It's Carla. Zac and Gwen want to get together to talk about the problem this evening. Are you free? Great. Why don't we meet down at one of the taverns in Pioneer Square?" There was a pause while Carla listened. "Okay, that sounds fine. I'll tell Gwen. See you later, Mason. Oh, by the way, I talked to a columnist from the *Review-Times* today. He covers art for the paper, and I got him interested in doing an interview with you. I think it could be a really nice piece of publicity, Mason. I'll let you know the details later. I think I'll have a chat with Theresa this afternoon too. I want to speak to her about putting *Frost* and *Mission* up front in the gallery. She's got them too far back. You need to lure people in with a flashy display. This is a competitive world, Mason. You can't run an art gallery the old-fashioned way. You need to catch people's attention. Yes, all right. See you then. Bye, Mason."

Guinevere took over her seat at her desk as her sister vacated it. "Does Mason mind the fact that you're beginning to run his career?"

"Not at all. He's grateful. He hates the business side of art."

"You don't seem to hate it."

"No," said Carla thoughtfully, "I love it. I think I could be very good at managing artists' careers, Gwen. I can see me now with my own little gallery in Pioneer Square. What do you think?"

"A fascinating idea. When do we meet Mason?"

"At five-thirty. Bouncer's. Know it? It's that little sidewalk tavern near the Midnight Light gallery."

"I know it. I'll tell Zac."

Carla was studying the tip of her pencil. "Why don't you and I leave a little early, Gwen? I want to talk to Theresa. We could go to the gallery first and then meet Mason and Zac."

"I don't know, Carla. I'm not sure I want to be around when you start lecturing Theresa on how to display Mason's art."

Carla smiled. "Leave it to me. I know what I'm doing."

"I wish I did." Guinevere picked up the phone to dial Zac's office.

As it happened, Guinevere was not obliged to go with Carla when she talked to Theresa that evening. The two sisters left Camelot Services and started walking up First Avenue toward Pioneer Square shortly before five. The street was full of commuters heading toward the ferry docks. In the mornings people who lived on Bainbridge Island or over in Bremerton frequently walked on board a ferry at one end and walked off to work in downtown Seattle at the other. In the evenings they reversed the procedure. The bars and pubs sprinkled along First Avenue catered to the people waiting for ferries or buses or those who simply wanted a little happy hour time before heading back to the suburbs. During the spring and summer many of the small taverns put tables out in front on the sidewalks.

Guinevere and Carla had crossed Yesler and were heading toward the Midnight Light gallery when someone hailed them from a sidewalk table. At first Guinevere didn't recognize the thin-faced man who was raising his hand to beckon them. Then something about his nervous, high-strung manner jolted her memory. She smiled aloofly at Henry Thorpe and was about to ignore his invitation when she thought better of the idea. She paused in front of his table.

"Hello, Henry. Carla, did you meet Henry Thorpe the other evening at Mason's show?"

"Yes, I believe I did," Carla said politely, waiting for her sister to continue down the street with her.

"Sit down, sit down," Thorpe commanded genially. He had obviously started happy hour early. The glass in front of him was half empty, and Guinevere was willing to bet it wasn't his first drink of the day. "Plenty of room. Let me buy you both a drink."

"We're in a hurry," Carla began austerely.

Guinevere looked at her. "Why don't you run along to the gallery, Carla? I'll have a quick drink with Henry and join you later."

"But, Gwen . . ." Carla paused, trying to read her sister's face. She seemed to realize that there was something going on and was shrewd enough not to interfere. With a smile for Henry she nodded and walked off.

"That sister of yours is nice-looking," Henry said, gazing after Carla with regret. "She ever do any modeling?"

"No." Guinevere ignored the fact that Henry had been hoping Carla would join him. She plunked herself down in the seat opposite him and smiled blandly. "I'll have a glass of white wine, please."

"What?" Henry was still gazing mournfully after Carla. "Oh, sure. White wine." After a couple of attempts he managed to catch the waitress's eye and give the order. Then he sat back, obviously resigning himself to a drink with the less attractive sister. "So. How goes the war?"

"What war?"

"Just an expression." Henry looked petulant. "Is Mason still riding high on his big success the other night?"

"He seems to be anxious to get back to work."

Thorpe's eyes narrowed. "It'll be interesting to see if he can get back to work. Lots of artists do great up until they start to make it big and then *phfft.* Up in smoke."

"I beg your pardon?" Guinevere sipped cautiously at her wine.

"They blow up. Dry up. Can't work anymore. Can't handle success. It's a common story," Thorpe explained knowledgeably.

"I hadn't realized." Perhaps this was the excuse Henry Thorpe had been trying to use for himself during the past few months, Guinevere thought. She remembered Mason saying that the thin, nervous man hadn't done any worthwhile painting for quite some time.

"Yeah. Some turn to coke, some head for the South Seas. Some just drink too much. Be interesting to see which route Adair uses."

"You're assuming he won't be able to handle his success. Perhaps you're wrong." Guinevere wasn't sure just why she had sat down with Henry Thorpe. Some vague instinct had suggested that she do so. Now she wondered if she hadn't wasted her time. Henry Thorpe was an embittered man who could only offer caustic comments about Mason Adair. It was a good thing Carla hadn't stayed.

"I'm not wrong," Thorpe said irritably. "You just wait and see. It's just like I told that guy a few months ago. Adair's a flash in the pan. Here today, gone tomorrow. By this time next year no one will remember him."

Guinevere caught her breath. "You told someone else that Mason probably wouldn't make it?"

Thorpe frowned and took a gulp of his drink. "Forget it. It was just some jerk hanging around the galleries looking to make a *discovery.* Thought he'd found one when he saw some of Adair's stuff hanging in the Midnight Light gallery. He happened to wander into the gallery next door where I had one of my pictures." Thorpe's mouth tightened. "One I did a while back. Still hasn't sold. Some fools don't know art when it hits them in the face. I thought for a while that this guy was going to buy it. But then he started talking about Adair's stuff."

Guinevere paused, trying to pick her words carefully. "But you set him straight on Mason Adair? Told him Mason wouldn't be important in the long run?"

Thorpe moved uneasily in his chair. "I just told him the truth, that's all. Said if he wanted to buy something worthwhile for his backer, he should be looking at someone else's pictures. Not Adair's."

"I see." Guinevere wished she'd had more experience trying to pump people. She would just have to rely on the empathic charm Zac claimed she had. "This man was buying for a backer? How interesting. Is a lot of art sold that way?"

"Oh, sure. People who don't trust their own taste use professionals to do their collecting for them." Thorpe was scathing.

"It does sound a little remote," Guinevere observed. "I'd certainly want to see what I was buying before making a purchase."

"Yeah, but a lot of people don't know one goddamn thing about art. They just want to *collect.*"

"I suppose so. Did this man end up buying anything by Adair?"

"I don't know. We talked for a while. Had a few drinks. He told me he thought he'd buy that picture I've got in the gallery next to Midnight Light. But he never did. I didn't see him after the night we had our drinks."

Guinevere wondered just how many drinks Henry Thorpe had put away while chatting with the art buyer's representative. She doubted whether Thorpe himself could remember, much less recall just how much he'd talked about Mason Adair to the man buying the drinks. "This happened a few months ago, you say?"

"Yeah. Six, maybe seven months. Say, you want another glass of wine?"

Guinevere smiled regretfully. "I wish I could stay, but I have an appointment."

"Oh." Thorpe looked disappointed.

"I think I'll stop in at the gallery next to Midnight Light and take a look at your painting," Guinevere said gently.

Thorpe brightened. "You do that. Who knows? Maybe you'll be the one to see the real depth in it." The momentary dash of hope died as he swallowed the last of his drink. "God knows no one else has. Everyone these days wants art to be *pretty.*"

"Thank you for the drink, Henry." Quietly Guinevere got up and left. She knew now why she had followed her instincts and let Henry Thorpe buy her a drink.

Farther down the block a sense of guilt made her drop in at the gallery next door to the Midnight Light gallery. She inquired about the Henry Thorpe painting and was shown a medium-size canvas hanging on the back wall.

The canvas was a ceremonial mask of rage and pain. It was done in harsh reds and browns, and it had a kind of raw energy that couldn't be denied. But Guinevere knew she certainly wouldn't want it hanging in her home. It was far too depressing.

With a sigh for the inner fury that must be driving Henry Thorpe, she walked back out onto the street. Zac would be waiting together with Carla and Mason at the tavern.

Zac was going to be fascinated to learn that not only had a big-time East Coast investor's representative been making inquiries about the people who used the Sandwick house for parties, but that an art buyer's representative had been making inquiries about Mason Adair. All at about the same time. Six or seven months ago.

Zac was highly suspicious of coincidences.

Chapter Eight

Clutching the simulated leather-bound document labeled *Analysis of Security Systems of Gallinger Industries* by Free Enterprise Security, Inc., Zac sat outside Elizabeth Gallinger's office door and awaited the Summons.

He had been sitting in the plush outer office for only a few minutes, but he had already used up his entire stock of bracing sayings and encouraging words. He was down to "A man's gotta do what a man's gotta do" and "No guts, no glory."

But the constant pep talk he had been feeding himself since he'd left his office fifteen minutes ago was not doing much to stem the tide of masculine nerves. He still wished he were anywhere but in Elizabeth Gallinger's outer office. The thought of facing her after the excruciatingly embarrassing scene on the terrace of her home last night was anathema. The thought of abandoning the potential fee he was about to receive for his security analysis services, however, was unthinkable. So: A man's gotta do what a man's gotta do.

He still wasn't quite ready when Elizabeth's private secretary smiled and showed him into the inner office, but he got another tiny reprieve. Elizabeth Gallinger was still on the phone.

"No, I don't think that's such a good idea. I want all four houses or none of them. See what you can do, Hal.

Yes, the usual financing arrangements. All right, that will be fine. Give me a call in the morning. Good-bye, Hal."

She hung up the phone and smiled brilliantly at Zac. "Sorry about that. Just finishing up some business with someone who handles my real estate investments for me. Do sit down, Zac. I see you have your report. I'm anxious to read it."

Zac breathed a sigh of relief. She was all business today. Maybe they could both just pretend last night's scene on the terrace hadn't happened. He took the leather chair across from her and handed her the genuine simulated leather binder. He could be all business too.

"I think you'll find that everything's been covered. I'll be glad to go over any of the details with the people in your security department, but in general they will concur with almost all the recommendations. I've already spoken to them. Your main areas of concern are the shipping docks and the computer operations. That's typical for companies the size of Gallinger Industries. But there are steps that can be taken to tighten up both departments. In addition, I've outlined some ways of limiting the kind of casual employee theft that takes place in large organizations."

Elizabeth opened the binder and glanced through the table of contents. Zac was enormously glad he'd taken Guinevere's advice and hired one of her temporary secretaries to type the final draft. At least he knew the document looked polished and professional. Of course, Guinevere had charged him a fortune for the afternoon's work, and it had been disconcerting to discover that the temporary secretary she had assigned him was male, but now it all seemed worthwhile. He waited while Elizabeth perused the opening remarks. Then she looked up with another smile.

"It looks fine, Zac. I certainly appreciate your efficiency.

I thought this sort of thing would take months to produce."

Not when you're inspired the way I was, Zac thought ruefully. "I gave it my top priority, Elizabeth."

"I see. Well, I suppose that concludes our association, doesn't it?" she asked with just the smallest touch of wistfulness.

Zac decided to steer clear of the direction in which she was heading. "I don't mean to pry, Elizabeth, but have you had a lot of experience in real estate investment? You said a moment ago that you were talking to your agent. I've, uh, been thinking of picking up a fixer-upper myself."

"Have you? It can be very time-consuming if you don't have someone like Hal to ride herd on the properties and financing for you."

"Financing? You don't just pay cash?"

Elizabeth shook her head. "Of course not. When you're investing, the whole point is to use other people's money as much as possible. Never tie up your own capital. If I can't work out a good financing arrangement with the owners or my bank, I don't buy."

"I see. I certainly appreciate the advice."

"Let me give you Hal's phone number. If you're really interested in picking up some choice properties, give him a call. He's a wonderful negotiator. Knows all the ins and outs of financing."

"Thank you, Elizabeth." Dutifully he accepted the phone number and inserted the slip of paper into his wallet. Then Zac got to his feet. "I've enjoyed working with you. I hope the analysis answers all your questions. As I said, give me a call if your people have any questions."

He was halfway to the door when Elizabeth's voice caught him. "Zac?"

His hand froze on the doorknob. "Yes, Elizabeth?" He glanced back over his shoulder.

"You won't reconsider the offer I made last night?"

Zac cleared his throat. "I'm afraid I can't. I've more or less committed my genes elsewhere."

There was a small hesitation, and then Elizabeth nodded soberly. "I understand. I envy her. Good-bye, Zac. And thank you." Regally gracious to the last.

"Good-bye, Elizabeth." He escaped into the outer office. Nodding politely to the secretary, he forced himself to walk calmly down the hall to the elevators. It seemed forever before the elevator doors hissed shut behind him and he was swept downstairs to safety.

Out on the street he breathed the air of freedom and glanced at his watch. He realized he was going to be a few minutes late to the rendezvous he'd arranged with Guinevere and Mason. He decided to grab one of the free buses that ran through the core of the city.

The bus was jammed because of the rush hour, and Zac nearly missed the stop he wanted in Pioneer Square. He emerged at last, straightening his jacket, and tried to look as if he'd just parked his Ferrari down the block. Hot-shot security consultants probably didn't ride buses, free or otherwise. Image.

Guinevere saw Zac approaching from the table she was sharing with Mason and Carla. The warm afternoon had attracted a good-size after-work crowd, and the sidewalk seating was nearly filled. She and Mason and Carla had been lucky to get a table.

"Over here, Zac." She waved encouragingly. "You're late."

"Sorry. Got held up at the office." He sat down beside her, nodding at Carla and Mason.

Guinevere waited impatiently while he ordered his tequila from the busy waiter, and then she leaned forward. "Okay, Zac. What's up? Have you made some major breakthroughs?"

He gave her a disparaging glance. "I called this little meeting to give us all a chance to hash over everything we've learned. No major breakthroughs. At least not from my end." He regarded the others with mild interest. "Has anyone else had any brilliant thoughts on the matter?"

Mason and Carla shook their heads unhappily. Guinevere smiled with smug expectancy. Zac eyed her warily. "Okay, Gwen. Why the cat-with-the-canary look?"

"Just a minor detail I picked up a little while ago from Henry Thorpe," she said easily.

"Who's Henry Thorpe?"

Quickly Guinevere explained.

"Thank you," Zac said gravely. "Always nice to be kept informed."

"You're welcome. Now to get on with this. He said that someone posing as an art dealer was hanging around the galleries a few months ago. He was asking questions about Mason Adair."

Zac was silent for a long moment while the others stared at Guinevere. "A few months ago," he finally repeated. "Would that have been at about the same time someone was posing as a real estate investor's representative and asking questions about the neighborhood where the Sandwick house is located?"

"You got it." Guinevere waited for praise and admiring comments on her brilliant detective work.

"Well, shit," Zac said.

Guinevere glared at him. "That wasn't quite what I expected."

Mason sighed. "I don't think that's such a big deal, Gwen. We know my cousin Dane has been trying to locate me for months. He must have hired private detectives, and they were probably the ones asking the questions."

Guinevere did a quick staccato drumroll of impatience with her crimson nails. "I suppose you're right."

Zac took over control of the discussion. "All right, we'll file that info for now. Mason, I've got a couple of questions. When you and your friends were sharing the good times at the Sandwick house did you install a big stone table and a wall of black velvet drapes in the basement?"

Mason looked startled. "Hell, no. Have you any idea what that would cost? Besides, we were into partying, not redecorating the basement. Did you say black velvet drapes?"

"Uh-huh."

"And a *stone* table?"

Zac nodded. "Looks something like an altar. A black altar."

Carla shivered. "It sounds gross."

Mason grimaced. "Actually, it sounds like something Baldric and Valonia might have installed. But where would they have gotten the cash? Real stone tables are incredibly expensive. Just ask in any good furniture store."

"They probably got the money for the table from the same place they got the cash to buy the house," Guinevere offered.

"I don't know," Mason said slowly. "They just didn't have that kind of cash. Not when I knew them."

"Perhaps they're into more profitable things these days," Zac suggested. "Drug dealing, maybe."

Mason thought about it. "I suppose it's a possibility. It would explain the sudden infusion of money. But you said there's no sign of them living in the house?"

"No," Zac admitted.

"Why would they buy a place and not live in it?" Carla wondered.

Guinevere shrugged. "They might have bought more than one house. Maybe they use one for their weird occult ceremonies and live elsewhere."

"The point is," Carla injected, "why are they hounding Mason?"

"Excellent point," Mason growled, taking a swallow of beer. "And what the hell are they doing with *Glare* stashed in the basement of that house?"

"You're sure neither one of them has any reason to hate you personally or to be professionally jealous?" Zac asked Mason.

The younger man shook his head dolefully. "Well, the group of us who were using the house originally refused to take their stupid ceremonies seriously. I suppose they could be resentful on that score. But why take it out on me?"

Guinevere frowned thoughtfully. "Because you're the only one they can find? Most of the others seem to have split for parts unknown."

"But there are a couple left in the area, and I haven't heard any gossip about them having the kind of trouble I'm having," Mason pointed out.

"Personally," declared Carla, "I still like the jealousy motive."

Zac shook his head. "It doesn't make any sense in this case, Carla. But your instincts are good."

"How's that?" she asked.

"You're looking for a rational motive. So am I. I would prefer one I could understand."

Guinevere said calmly, "I think the witchcraft is a potentially genuine motive. There have been occasional newspaper articles about occult groups living in the Northwest. This wouldn't be a first. There are some strange people in this world, Zac."

"I know," he agreed. "But, like Carla, I guess I would prefer a more rational motive."

"If someone were after money, why haven't they tried to blackmail me or tell me the vandalism will stop if I pay them off?" Mason asked, wrinkling his brow.

"How could you pay them off?" Guinevere asked bluntly. "You've been living at borderline poverty level for over two years. A couple of sales at the gallery show the other night aren't enough to put you on easy street."

The question hung in the air. In silence the four people

sitting around the table finished their drinks as the after-work crowd began to thin. Finally Zac got to his feet with an abrupt movement.

"Let's go home, Gwen. I've got some thinking to do." He turned around and started making his way between tables.

Guinevere threw the other two an apologetic look as she got hurriedly to her feet. "Sorry. He gets this way sometimes when he goes into Deep Think."

"Deep Think?" Mason stared after the departing Zac. "He's thinking?"

"Uh-huh. See you later, both of you. I'll let you know if he comes up with any brilliant ideas this evening."

Guinevere trotted after Zac, catching up with him as he started down the sidewalk toward her apartment. He had his hands shoved into his jacket pockets, his shoulders slightly hunched, and the remote, miles-away look in his eyes that Guinevere had come to associate with times such as this. She didn't bother trying to ask any questions. Zac would talk when he was ready. Silently she walked beside him until they reached her apartment building.

Upstairs she poured him another shot of tequila and sat beside him on the sofa while he cradled the drink in both hands and stared unseeingly out of one of her vaulted windows.

This mood could last for hours, Guinevere reminded herself. She might as well fix something to eat. Rising to her feet again, she traipsed back into the kitchen to make a sandwich. No sense wasting gourmet cooking on Zac when he was in Deep Think.

Three more hours passed before Zac finally spoke. Guinevere, deep into a mystery at the time, was startled. She had gotten accustomed to the silence.

"Those private investigators were asking their questions several months ago," he began slowly, just as if there had been no break in the conversation.

"About six or seven months ago," Guinevere agreed.

"Yet cousin Dane doesn't contact Adair until this week."

Guinevere closed her book. "That's true."

"Why the delay?" Zac asked softly. "Those investigators must have gotten their answers six months ago. They must have located Adair then. He wasn't trying to hide. He hadn't even changed his name. Once someone had realized he was in Seattle and was part of the local art scene, the rest would have been easy. Cousin Dane and the rest of the family must have known where he was six months ago."

"Zac, what has Dane Fitzpatrick's search for Mason got to do with the Sandwick house and the vandalism?"

Zac picked up one of the sandwiches that had been sitting on a plate in front of him for the past three hours. "I told you earlier that given a choice, I prefer a rational motive. Money is the most rational of all motives. There's money in this mess, Gwen. It's all over the place. Fifty-five thousand in cash to buy a run-down house on Capitol Hill with virtually no negotiation. Real estate wheeler-dealers always negotiate, and they don't use their own cash if they can avoid it."

Guinevere eyed him curiously. "You're an authority on the subject?"

"No, but I talked to an authority this afternoon."

"Who?"

"Elizabeth Gallinger. She was on the phone to the guy who handles her real estate investments when I walked into her office."

"I see." Guinevere decided this wasn't the time to discuss Queen Elizabeth in greater detail. "Okay, so there's money in this mess. It could be drug money, as you suggested earlier, Zac. Drug dealers with a lot of excess cash on their hands might not quibble over the price of a house they want to buy."

Zac nodded. "True. But that isn't the only money involved here. There's East Coast preppy money too."

"Adair family money? But that doesn't make any sense. Mason's out of his father's will. And how would Baldric and Valonia know about his family connections, anyway?"

"An interesting question."

"Zac, what's going on? What are you thinking?"

"Nothing solid yet. But there are some things I'm going to have to check on tomorrow. Things I probably should have checked out much earlier." He munched his sandwich and then looked at Guinevere. "Let's go to bed, honey. I've got a lot to do in the morning."

On the way into the bedroom Zac yawned hugely and said, "This isn't so bad, is it?"

"What isn't so bad?"

"Living together."

She slid him a speculative glance. "We haven't exactly given it a long run," she reminded him cautiously. "This was just a short-term arrangement until you solve Mason's problem."

"I know." Complacently he walked into the bedroom and started unbuttoning his shirt. "But the concept has potential, don't you think? Of course, if we did this on a full-time basis, you'd have to get rid of that lousy coffee machine."

Guinevere, not knowing how to respond to the hint that Zac might actually want to move in with her, sought refuge in humor. "I hope you won't force me to choose between that beautiful machine and you, Zac. It would be a tough choice. The coffee machine is color-coordinated to my apartment, don't forget."

"And I'm not?" He finished undressing and crawled into bed beside her.

She touched his broad shoulder as he turned out the light beside the bed. Then she smiled. "Not exactly. But you do have your uses."

His feet tangled with hers as Zac pulled her close. "I'm damn well more useful than that imported coffee maker. Come here and use me."

Guinevere went into his arms the way she always did, with a sensual abandon that forever surprised her and which Zac inevitably accepted with deep hunger.

It wasn't just the money and the motive that raised questions, Zac told himself the next morning as he sat in his office and went over his notes on the Mason Adair situation. There was also the curious matter of timing. The Sandwick house had been sold at about the same time that an unknown investigator or investigators were asking for information on Adair. At least one of those phantom private detectives had said he was representing an East Coast real estate investor and had specifically asked about the Sandwick house.

Money and timing. In the security business those two issues often went together. One was usually related to the other. Zac stared at his notepad a while longer, and then he reached out and picked up the phone.

"Camelot Services." The professionally cheerful voice on the other end of the line was not Guinevere's.

"Hi, Carla, it's Zac. Is your sister there?"

"Nope. She's out drumming up business with a new client. What can I do for you?"

"Since when does she have to leave the office to drum up business?" He glanced at his watch. "I was going to take her to lunch."

"Well, you'll have to get in line. The new client is taking her to lunch. I think he intends to set up a contract with Camelot Services to provide his firm with all the temps he needs. He'll get priority service that way."

"I don't see why Gwen has to have lunch with him in order to settle the deal." Zac was aware of the fact that he was growling.

"You know how it is with these executives," Carla said vaguely. "They do everything over lunch."

Zac had a sudden jolting image of what "everything" might include and immediately shoved it out of his mind. Guinevere had a business to run, after all. He couldn't afford to get nervous every time she had lunch with a client. "All right, Carla. Tell her I called. In the meantime can you do me a favor?"

"You want another typist?"

"At the prices Camelot Services charges? Not on your life. It will take me six months to pay the bill on the last one I got from your sister."

"Gwen believes in turning a profit whenever possible," Carla admitted blandly.

"And after all I've done for that woman," Zac intoned.

"I'll let you two settle the matter of the bill for the typist we sent over. What was the favor?"

"I need Mason's father's phone number back East."

Carla sucked in her breath. "His father's phone number? But, Zac, why?"

"I don't know why. Not yet. I'm just trying to tie some loose ends together. Can you get it from him for me?"

"Possibly. But he'll ask a hundred questions, and I can't blame him. What shall I tell him?"

"Tell him I need it to pursue his case," Zac said, irritated at the delay. "If he wants me to stay on it, he'd better cooperate."

"Okay, okay, don't get huffy. I'll contact him now." Carla hung up the phone.

Zac sat with his feet propped on his desk, leaned back in his swivel chair, and waited. While he waited, he stared into the office across the hall. The sales rep who was using the other cubicle as a base for his operations finally sensed the steady gaze and glanced up questioningly. Zac looked away, wishing he had a real window. One of these days he was going to have to move up in the world. He needed a bigger and better office. A few more accounts like the Gallinger account and maybe he'd be able to afford one.

The phone rang five minutes later. It was Carla. "All right, Zac, I've got it for you." She rattled it off while he copied it down. "Mason wanted to know what you were going to do. I told him not to worry, that you would be discreet and not become involved in what was obviously a private family matter."

"You told him all that?"

"I certainly did. Mason's very touchy on the subject of his family. It's a very unhappy situation, you know. I reassured him that you would be very careful about what you said to his father. Don't make a liar out of me, Zac."

Carla hung up the phone before he could ask if Guinevere had returned yet from her client lunch. He looked down at the phone number he had written in his notebook and wondered if he couldn't wait until after five o'clock to make the call. He hated to pay daytime long-distance rates when there wasn't a client footing the expense tab. With a resigned sigh he picked up the phone and dialed.

It took a great deal of talking to get Julius Edward Adair on the telephone. Apparently Mr. Adair was not the sort of man who took phone calls from strangers, especially strangers on the West Coast. But after Zac mentioned Mason's name a few times, the senior Adair came on the line. The rich, deep voice was full of East Coast prep-school breeding. Zac ignored his own annoyed reaction. It wasn't Adair's fault that he came from a family that could trace its lineage and its money back a couple of centuries. Everyone had a cross to bear.

"Mr. Adair? This is Zachariah Justis. I'm president of a firm called Free Enterprise Security, Inc. We have been asked to make some inquiries on behalf of your son, Mason."

There was a moment of shocked silence. "Mason? What

do you know about my son? Where is he? Where did you say you were calling from? Oregon?"

"Washington, sir."

"My son is in Washington, D.C.?"

"No, sir, State of."

"The State of Washington? Good Lord. Whatever made him go there?"

"This may come as a jolt, Mr. Adair, but out here we really don't think of Washington as being just the last stop for the wagon trains any longer. We've even got flush toilets in a few of the more progressive homes now."

"There is no need for sarcasm, Mr. . . . What did you say your name was?"

Zac took a deep breath. "Justis. Zachariah Justis."

"And you say you're working for my son?"

"I'm making a few inquiries on his behalf, yes, sir."

"May I talk to him?" Adair asked carefully.

"I'm sorry, he's not here at the moment."

"Will you give me his phone number, please," Adair said imperiously.

"I can't do that," Zac said with sudden gentleness. "He hasn't authorized me to do so. But I would have thought you had that information already. Or at least his address."

"How on earth would I have that? We haven't been able to locate Mason for quite some time. I've had men working on the problem for almost a year."

Zac cleared his throat, hunching a little over the phone while he reached for his notepad. "Have you, sir? You, personally, commissioned a firm of private investigators to find him?"

"I had my nephew handle the details, but, yes, we've been trying to locate him. Now, if you have information on the matter, Mr. Justis, I will be more than happy to pay for it."

Zac winced at the cold condescension in the words. "Sir,

there would be a slight conflict of interest at the moment. I'm already working for your son."

"What are you doing for him? Is he in trouble? What does he need?" There was a father's genuine concern beneath the cultured, aloof exterior.

"What he needs and what I need in order to help him are some answers, Mr. Adair."

"I don't know who you are, Mr. Justis, but I can find out. In the meantime, if you have made contact with my son, I don't want to lose contact with you. Ask your questions."

"I'm afraid I will be making some extremely personal inquiries, sir."

"Just ask, damn it!"

"All right. I understand that you struck Mason out of your will a couple of years ago when the two of you quarreled."

"That is correct," Adair said austerely. "I assumed it would bring him to his senses. Mason had been born and bred with a silver spoon in his mouth. Frankly, I didn't think he'd last more than three or four months without access to the kind of money and connections he had always taken for granted. I have realized during the past couple of years that I was mistaken. That boy turned out to be every damn bit as stubborn as I am. In some ways it made me realize that he was a throwback to his grandfather and his great-grandfather. Mason has lived a soft life, but it seems my son is not soft because of it." Pride laced the comment.

"You say Mason had always lived in relative luxury?"

"It was his heritage. In return he had an obligation to that heritage. We . . . disagreed on the subject."

"I understand." Zac paused and then asked his next question. "You say you've been trying to contact him for some time now."

"That is correct."

"Did you intend to put Mason back in your will in the event that you located him?"

"Yes, Mr. Justis. I did."

Zac exhaled slowly. "I think that answers most of my questions, Mr. Adair."

"Wait, don't hang up, Justis," Adair said urgently. "What about Mason?"

"I'll tell him I talked to you and that you've been trying to reach him," Zac said, searching for a way to leave the older man some hope without building those hopes too high.

"May I have your number, Mr. Justis?"

"Yes." Zac gave it to him and then eased himself off the phone. He sat for a long while after that, contemplating what he had learned. He had been right about this mess. There was money involved. A lot of it. Adair money.

Things finally began to jell. It didn't take any great intuition to realize that there was more at stake than a bit of malicious mischief.

Dane Fitzpatrick had located Mason several months ago, but he not only hadn't contacted the artist, he also hadn't bothered to tell Mason's father. Furthermore, Dane had made a trip to the West Coast and actually talked to Mason. Then he'd returned home and still not mentioned the fact to the senior Adair. Was it because Mason was still being stubborn and refused to talk to his father?

Or because once contact was made, Mason would be back in the will and Dane would be out in the cold?

And what the hell did all this have to do with Baldric, Valonia, and the Sandwick house?

Zac dialed Guinevere's number again, but Carla assured him that she was still engaged at lunch. Zac frowned as he glanced at his watch. It was already after two. How long was the business lunch going to last? He had another appointment, himself, that afternoon, one that would take him out of the office. "Carla, tell her to call me as soon as she walks in the door, understand? I want to talk to her."

"I'll tell her, Zac."

The phone was ringing as Guinevere walked into her office much later that afternoon. Carla had already left for the day, she noted, glancing at her sister's messages on the desk. Apparently she'd scheduled a meeting with Theresa at the Midnight Light gallery. Guinevere picked up the receiver.

"Camelot Services."

"Gwen, is that you? I've got to talk to you." Mason Adair's voice was hoarse with tension.

"Mason? What's the problem?"

"I'll tell you when I see you. I'm in my studio. Please come quickly. Something else has happened. I can't reach Zac." He replaced the receiver on his end.

The phone hummed in Guinevere's ear. She stared at it, frowning. The urgency in Mason's voice had been real. Guinevere paused long enough to dial Zac's number, but when Gertie answered, she just said to tell Zac she'd called and then hung up. Guinevere grabbed her shoulder bag and hurried out the door.

Chapter Nine

Guinevere had almost reached Mason's apartment building when a hunch made her hesitate beside her own door. The urgency in Mason's voice had alarmed her. She had a feeling that whatever had happened was something Zac would want to know about.

Digging her key out of her purse, she let herself inside her own building, determined to try to reach Zac by telephone before going on to Mason's apartment. The call from her phone would only delay her another minute or two.

She opened her door, intent only on calling from the kitchen phone. The mini-blinds on her kitchen window were open and she peered through them, trying to see if she could spot Mason across the street. There was no sign of him.

Zac's phone was once more answered by his service.

"I'm sorry, Mr. Justis is not available at the moment. May I take a message?"

"Gertie, this is Guinevere Jones. Just tell him I called again and that I'd like him to contact me or Mason Adair as soon as he gets back."

"I'll tell him, Gwen. Listen, are you all right? You sound a little upset."

"No, I'm fine, Gertie. Just fine. Be sure to give Zac my message."

"I will."

"Thanks." Guinevere hung up the phone and heard the faint noise in the hall at the same time. Belatedly she realized that she hadn't locked the door behind her when she entered the apartment. She had only intended to stay a moment or two.

Nerves. Gertie was right. She was a little upset and there was no good reason. The worst Mason might have to tell her about was another incident of vandalism.

Hoisting her purse over her shoulder again, she swung around . . . and came to a dead halt as she found herself facing a thick, heavily built man with a gun clutched in his right fist. Shock held her paralyzed for about three taut seconds. It hit her quite forcibly that this was the man she had seen through Mason's window the night he had been attacked. He wasn't wearing a hood this time, and his scraggly, limp brown hair hung almost to his shoulders. There was a flat, aggressive bluntness in his features that reminded her of a pit bulldog. But it was the wild, alien look in his washed-out eyes that truly frightened her.

"Don't say a word. Not one single word. I can kill you and be out of this building before any of your neighbors realize what's happened. In fact, most of them aren't even home at this time of day. I already checked. You understand me, Guinevere Jones?"

"I understand." She stood very still. There was something abnormal about the way her blood was moving in her veins. Her pulse seemed too fast all of a sudden. Her fingers were tightly clenched around the strap of her shoulder bag. "What do you want?"

"We've already got what we want, don't we, Valonia?"

"Yes." The woman who materialized behind the heavy man had a ghostlike paleness about her that was unnerving under the circumstances. In contrast to the man, she was very thin with pale skin, pale eyes, colorless lips, and wispy, almost red hair that hung nearly to her waist. She stared at Guinevere with an unblinking, intent gaze. She held a small package in one hand. "So. We were right to keep an eye on this building too. You were correct in assuming she might stop here before going over to *his* place."

Guinevere forced her tongue to work again. "His place? Mason's? What have you done with him? What's going on here? Look, I don't know what this is all about, but it's obvious you two are playing some pretty serious games; games that have gone much too far. If you had any sense, you'd get out of here. Now."

"Games?" The man, who must have been Baldric, smiled without any humor. "You think we're playing games? You're a fool. But that's not very strange, considering the fact that most people are fools. You should never have gotten involved, Guinevere Jones. Your foolishness is going to cost you. Come here."

Guinevere didn't move. For some reason her attention was on the thin woman. She was holding the small package in her hand with a tension that Guinevere could feel across the width of the kitchen. Even as Guinevere watched, Valonia raised her hand slightly. A strange scent wafted through the air.

"I'm not going anywhere, and if you try to drag a struggling woman down the stairs and out the front door, you're going to be asking for trouble. Someone's going to notice and you know it."

"We do not intend to drag a struggling woman out onto the street," Valonia assured her, stepping closer and raising the oddly scented package. It appeared to be a folded cloth, part of which was dangling into a jar fashioned of cobalt-blue glass. Liquid from the glass was climbing the trail of fabric, permeating it. "You will not be struggling at all. And we will be certain to take you down the back stairs. No one will see you, Guinevere Jones. Do not deceive yourself with false hope. There is no hope."

The acrid smell emanating from the cloth and the glass in Valonia's hand was stronger now. Guinevere was suddenly more afraid of it than she was of the weapon Baldric was holding. She edged backward and found herself up against the counter. The handsome red-and-black coffee machine was immediately behind her.

"Don't touch me," Guinevere hissed. "Don't you dare touch me, you little witch."

Valonia smiled evilly. "How very astute of you." She lunged forward, trying to slap the package against Guinevere's nose and mouth. Guinevere gasped and tried to dodge. Her arm swept out in a wide, desperate arc in an attempt to ward off Valonia.

"Stand still or I'll shoot!" Baldric issued the warning as he leapt toward Guinevere.

Guinevere's hand missed Valonia but struck the coffee machine. Her fingers closed around the handle of the glass pot just as Baldric clamped a hand around her mouth and shoved the snout of the gun into her ribs. The smell of the object in Valonia's hand was overpowering. The damp cloth was forced against Guinevere's nose. Almost instantly her senses reeled.

"Hold her still!" Valonia shoved the cloth more tightly into position.

"Watch out for that coffeepot," Baldric snarled as Guinevere swung her arm in a frantic, awkward movement.

From a great distance Guinevere heard the sound of shattering glass and Baldric's furious oath. She wasn't sure if she had hit either of them. Already she was slumping to the floor, her mind spinning away into darkness as the fumes from the cloth invaded her consciousness. She was aware of a great deal of scrambling movement and crude oaths from both Baldric and Valonia as they tried to follow her to the floor. Guinevere lost her frail grip on the handle of the pot.

She scrambled about in useless protest as she tried to evade Baldric's grasp. Both Baldric and Valonia were concentrating on keeping the cloth pressed against her face.

They didn't pay any attention to Guinevere's futile struggles. When her hand closed around a shard of heavy coffeepot glass, Guinevere was too far gone even to be sure of what she was holding. Some vague, rapidly receding instinct made her fumble the piece of glass into the pocket of her skirt. She wondered fleetingly if it would fall out when Baldric and Valonia carried her down the fire escape stairs, and then she wondered what she could possibly do with a piece of glass in any event. Useless effort.

"Clean up that mess." Baldric's order seemed to come from a million miles away. "We don't want anyone to guess what happened here. Get rid of the glass. Hurry!"

It occurred to Guinevere as she slipped into unconsciousness that Zac, for one, would be glad to know that the stylish coffee machine was out of commission, at least temporarily.

Zac sat brooding in Guinevere's apartment, a glass of tequila in front of him. It was nearly eight o'clock. He knew that beyond a shadow of a doubt because he'd been glancing at his watch every couple of minutes for the past two hours. He was not in a good mood. The only explanation he could come up with for Guinevere's absence was that lunch with the client had turned into dinner. That explanation did not please him.

In fact, Zac decided, staring at the half empty tequila glass, the explanation infuriated him. He sat alone on the black leather sofa and faced the extent of his jealousy. This was what came of not pushing her for some formal commitment. Declaring to each other that they were in the midst of a genuine affair was not enough. Something more was needed in this relationship. Zac vowed that when Guinevere finally came through the front door, he would point that out to her in no uncertain terms.

Grand, masculine wisdom told him that women had become unmanageable during the twentieth century. Somehow, somewhere, sometime, men were going to have to put their feet down again and exert a little male authority. It was ridiculous that a woman, even a businesswoman, could take an extended lunch with a client and then turn around and take an extended dinner with him too.

The phone rang as Zac was mentally listing his grievances. Irritated, he stood up, scooped up the glass of tequila, and went into the kitchen to answer it. The voice on the other end was Carla's.

"Hi, Zac. Is Guinevere there?"

"No, she is not. Apparently lunch turned into dinner."

"What does that mean?"

"I haven't seen her since this morning. Every time I called Camelot Services today, you informed me she was at lunch with a prime client. Remember?"

"I remember. You sound annoyed, Zac."

"Possibly because I am annoyed. It is eight o'clock at night and I still haven't seen your sister."

"Hmmm. She should have been home by now."

"Tell me about it." He took a swallow of tequila.

"Well, we can commiserate together," Carla said with an air of resignation. "I can't locate Mason, either. We were supposed to have dinner together. I was going to coach him on how to handle the interview with the reporter from the *Review-Times.* Maybe he got caught up in his work."

Zac's brows came together in a heavy line as he considered that bit of information. Automatically he glanced through the mini-blinds to check Mason's studio. The window was unlit, but there was still enough lingering daylight to let him see that the apartment across the street was empty. "He's not working. I can see the studio from here."

There was a pause from Carla's end of the phone. "Interesting. I wonder where he could be? Do you suppose he and Guinevere have, uh, gone out to dinner together?"

"Why would they do that? Especially if Mason had a date with you?"

"I don't know," Carla admitted.

There was another long pause as they both considered the various possibilities. Zac's frown deepened. "Hang up, Carla. I want to call my answering service. I didn't do it earlier because I got back to the office late this afternoon and I didn't want to deal with any business until tomorrow morning."

"Doesn't Gertie have Gwen's number?"

"Yes, but she wouldn't necessarily try to contact me here unless I gave her specific instructions to do so. Hang up. I want to check."

"Okay. Zac, let me know if you find either of them."

"I will." Zac cut the connection and redialed. "Gertie? This is Zac. Any messages?"

"Gwen called around five o'clock. Said to tell you to contact either her or Mason Adair when you got back to the office. I tried your office around five-fifteen and again at five-thirty. You weren't there. I thought you would call in before now." Gertie sounded defensive.

Zac rubbed the back of his neck while he contemplated Mason's empty studio. "Don't worry about it, Gertie. Did she say where she was when she called?"

"I'm afraid not, Mr. Justis."

"All right. Thanks for the message." He let the receiver drop into the cradle. If Gwen hadn't stipulated where he was supposed to call, then he had to assume that she had been calling from either her office or her apartment. She was in neither of those locations now. And Mason Adair was not in his studio.

Uneasily Zac gazed around the kitchen, wondering if Gwen had been standing here when she made the call. It was a possibility. He stood silently, aware of the utter lack of Gwen's presence. Where the hell could she be at this hour of the night? Surely she and Adair hadn't decided that they were more than two ships passing in the night, after all. It didn't make any sense. There was no way on earth Gwen could respond in bed the way she did to him, Zac told himself, and then turn around and jump into Mason Adair's arms.

Besides, he'd seen the way Adair had looked at Carla the last time they were together. The artist definitely had his eye on the younger Jones sister.

Damn it, Zac thought, *I'm letting my imagination run wild.* Maybe what he needed was another shot of tequila. His eyes went to the cupboard that held the Jose Cuervo, and for some reason he noticed that the coffee machine was minus its pot.

No loss, Zac told himself as he glanced around the small room, looking for it. With any luck the sucker was broken and Gwen wouldn't be able to replace it. It would be tough to find a replacement for that idiotically designed pot. Out of curiosity he opened the cupboard under the sink and saw the broken pieces of glass in the trash can. He could imagine Gwen's irritation. She had really liked the looks of that coffee machine.

He sniffed and wrinkled his nose. He could do Gwen a favor and empty her trash. It was getting a little strong. Zac reached down and pulled the plastic sack out of the can. Another unpleasant whiff made him turn his head the other way and twist the top of the bag firmly shut.

Zac was halfway to the door when he realized that, as unpleasant as the smell was, it didn't remind him in any way of garbage. He paused and cautiously opened the sack. He couldn't identify the odor, and that was beginning to bother him. It seemed to cling most strongly to a couple of pieces of paper towel. Perhaps Guinevere had spilled something and used the paper towels to wipe up the mess or clean her hands. But Zac couldn't think of anything she had around the apartment that would give off this acrid, penetrating odor. Thoughtfully he closed the bag and went out into the hall to dump it down the garbage chute.

When he was finished, he locked Guinevere's door and headed for Mason's apartment. There might be something there that would give him a hint of where Mason, at least, had gone.

But Adair's apartment was as empty as it had looked from Guinevere's window. After letting himself inside Zac spent a few minutes wandering around, trying to understand the new sense of tension he was feeling. He was near Adair's worktable when he caught the faint trace of the same smell he had discovered in Gwen's trash can.

Zac came to an abrupt halt, a painful sense of alertness jolting through him. For a few seconds he stood quite still. Then he went to work, looking for the source of the smell. A few minutes later he realized it was lingering around the workbench, itself, as though something had been spilled on the paint-stained wood and had dried. He leaned closer and inhaled carefully.

His head swam sickeningly for a few seconds. Stepping back, Zac turned and went through the apartment with quick, long steps. Nothing. Absolutely nothing except that damned odor.

Guinevere and Mason had disappeared, and both had probably been in their own apartments as recently as late this afternoon. The lingering odor was the only link.

Zac closed his eyes briefly, trying to fight back the knowledge that he knew he couldn't avoid. Then he reached for Adair's phone to call Carla's Capitol Hill apartment.

"Carla? Any word?"

"You mean from Mason? No. Zac, what's wrong?"

"I don't know. Look, I'm going to call Gertie and tell her to ring your number if she gets any more messages."

"All right, but why, Zac?"

"I'm not sure yet," he said honestly. "But I want to do

some looking around. If you don't hear from me by midnight, I want you to contact the police. Tell them everything you know about the mess Adair's in and have them check out the Sandwick place. Got that?"

"Yes, but, Zac, what's *wrong?*"

"Nothing, I hope."

But he wasn't feeling so hopeful as he placed the call to Gertie and then loped downstairs to where he'd parked the Buick. He drove first to his own apartment in a tower of condominiums that overlooked Elliott Bay. Leaving the Buick in the loading zone, he took the elevator to the ninth floor.

He was getting accustomed to living with Guinevere's bright color scheme, Zac realized absently as he retrieved his small Beretta from under the bathroom sink. The subdued browns and grays of his own apartment seemed dull to him now. Then, again, life in general would seem very dull without Guinevere Jones.

On the other hand, he decided grimly, going swiftly down the hall to the elevators, she didn't have to go these lengths to liven things up for him.

The decision to check out the Sandwick house was based as much on guesses and a hunch as on anything else. But Zac had relied on such a nonscientific approach often enough in the past. He just wished to hell he'd started putting the guesses together into a hunch before now. As usual he'd been a little slow getting to the final conclusion. Now he had to make certain Guinevere didn't pay for his slowness.

During the drive to the house on Capitol Hill, Zac was aware of two things. One was that it was almost dark now. The other was that he was calming down as his mind and body slipped into the familiar, cold, savagely alert state. He knew this condition, and he didn't like it. It was almost painful. He'd experienced it too often in the past. He'd assumed that when he'd left his job with the international security firm and started his own business, he would never again know this kind of acute awareness. What could be so dangerous about analyzing white-collar business security problems?

It only went to show, Zac decided, that life was full of surprises.

Guinevere wasn't sure she had regained consciousness. She knew she had her eyes open, but the oppressive darkness surrounding her was as thick and menacing as that which she had known when she'd passed out.

She was aware of an uncomfortable, binding feeling on her wrists and ankles and finally decided she must have been tied hand and foot. The floor on which she lay was cold and damp.

At least there wasn't a gag across her mouth. But that was probably because no one would hear if she chose to scream. She lay still for a moment, listening. She thought she heard someone else's steady breathing.

"Is anyone there?" Her throat felt dry and raspy.

"Gwen? Are you awake?"

"Mason. My God, where are you?"

"A few feet away from you, I think. I can't move. They've got me tied up."

"Are you all right?"

"Yeah, I think so. What a fool I was. Zac was right. I should have let him go to the cops."

"I'm not sure it would have done much good. Who could have predicted things would turn this nasty? We all assumed it was just a case of harassment and vandalism." She struggled to find a slightly more comfortable position and felt something scrape against her thigh. "My head hurts."

"Mine too. Probably from that stuff they used to knock us out."

"We're talking about Valonia and Baldric, right?"

"Afraid so," Mason agreed wearily. "I got back to my studio this afternoon and found another painting defaced. I called Zac, and when there was no answer, I called you. As soon as I hung up the phone, they jumped me. They must have been hiding in the bathroom."

"Have they gone crazy?"

"Looks like it. I told you, they always did take that damned occult stuff too seriously. I think they've gone absolutely bonkers."

"Where are we?"

"I'm not sure," Mason admitted, "but at a guess, I'd say it's the basement of the Sandwick house."

"Good grief." The object in her skirt pocket poked through the fabric, making Guinevere wince. She tugged at the skirt with her bound hands, trying to pull the pocket out of the way. When she got a grip on the fabric, she suddenly remembered that she had put something in that pocket just before she'd gone unconscious. Laboriously she inched the skirt around her waist until she could get her fingers into the pocket. She touched the heavy shard of glass. "Hmmm."

"What's wrong?"

"Everything. But I just found a piece of glass. In the movies people always seem able to cut through their bonds with handy little things such as this."

"Maybe if I can get closer to you, I can help. It's damn sure worth a try."

Guinevere heard him shift about in the darkness, trying to maneuver himself toward the sound of her voice. "Over here," she whispered.

"Keep talking. I can't see a thing."

Guinevere turned on her side, trying for a better angle of attack against the ropes that bound her. Her face brushed fabric, and she sucked in her breath in alarm.

"What is it?"

"Just fabric. Feels like velvet. Must be the drapes Zac

told us about." She went to work on the ropes again. It didn't take long before she realized that in spite of what happened in the movies, cutting through tough rope with a piece of glass was neither a speedy nor a simple proposition.

"What do you think they're going to do with us, Gwen?"

"That," answered Guinevere with great depth of feeling, "is something I don't want to think about. The real question is how long it's going to take Zac to realize something's wrong."

"Even if he does realize it, how can he put two and two together and figure out where we are?"

"Zac is very good at putting two and two together. Eventually."

Zac took his usual route through the weed-strewn, languishing backyards that were such a prominent feature on the dilapidated block of old houses. There were lights on in one or two of the structures, but for the most part everything looked as vacant at this hour of the evening as it did at three in the morning. A fat gray cat meowed questioningly at him, and he thought he recognized the animal as belonging to Abby Kettering but he couldn't be sure. It disappeared in search of more interesting night prey.

From the shelter of the precariously tilting garage of the house next door to the Sandwick place, Zac stood watching for a time. There were no lights on in the Sandwick house, even though it was dark, but there was activity. Occasionally he thought he caught the brief flicker of a flashlight. It never lasted long. Whoever was in the house was depending mainly on the limited light from the street. They obviously did not want to attract attention.

Of course, Zac reminded himself, down in the basement they could have all the light they wanted. No one would ever be aware of it. No one would be aware of anything that went on in that basement. Not for a long time.

As he watched, a long-haired, burly figure dressed in pants and what appeared to be a sweatshirt moved along the side of the house, heading toward the kitchen door. With that long stride it was probably a man. The kitchen door opened and closed behind him.

Zac waited a few more minutes and then eased forward, hugging what cover he could find. When he reached the Sandwick house, he stayed in the shadows near the kitchen door and paused again, listening. The faint sound of voices came from inside the darkened kitchen, but he couldn't make out the words.

He waited until the voices stopped. The next sound was of a heavy door being opened and closed inside the kitchen. Zac knew it had to be the door to the basement. Silence reigned.

Zac was about to let himself into the kitchen and deal with whatever he found there when a faint scraping sound made him halt. The kitchen door swung open, and a man stepped out to look around. The figure was dressed in a dark robe, the cowl of which was pulled forward, almost completely concealing the face. The hem of the garment fell to his sandaled feet.

Zac didn't hesitate. He stepped forward quickly as the hooded figure glanced in the other direction. The other man never made a sound as Zac snapped the heel of his hand against his throat. Zac caught his victim as the dazed man sank slowly toward the ground. With any luck he wasn't unconscious, just temporarily voiceless.

The robed figure was heavy, but when Zac dragged him into the concealment provided by a tree at the back of the yard, he knew the guy wasn't heavy enough to be the same man as the one who had surprised him in the basement. Zac twisted his arm around the dazed man's throat and held the nose of the Beretta against his neck, making sure his victim felt the cold steel as he groaned and opened his eyes.

"What the hell . . . ? Who are you?"

Zac reached out and shoved back the hood. "Strangely enough, I was going to ask you the same question. But not now."

"If you're police, you got no business here. This is a private religious ceremony. We aren't doing anything wrong."

"Sure. Unfortunately for you, I'm not from the police. Now tell me exactly what is going on in that place and tell me quickly. Start with your job. What the hell are you supposed to be doing all dressed up like something out of the Middle Ages?"

"I don't have to tell you a damned thing!"

"True, but if you don't, I'll slit your throat and try someone else who might be a little more cooperative." Zac kept the gun in place while he flicked open the pocketknife he held in his other hand. He sensed the man's startled reaction. A knife against the throat sometimes had more impact than a gun. Zac wasn't sure why this should be so, but he'd seen the phenomenon before this.

"You wouldn't . . . you can't . . . Look, I don't know what you want, but you got no business here. We aren't hurtin' anything."

Zac let the tip of the blade sink into a few layers of skin. He knew he drew a little blood. "One more time. Like I said, if you're not feeling chatty, I'll get rid of you and try someone else."

Something about his voice must have gotten through to the man. Zac had seen that phenomenon before too. Perhaps it was because the utter lack of emotion in the words told the victim very clearly that Zac would carry out the threat. Zac knew he lacked Guinevere's empathic charm, but there were other ways to communicate.

"Look, I'm just the doorman, you know? I keep watch

on the door before the ceremony starts. Make sure only members get inside. That's all."

"And that's what you're supposed to do tonight?"

"Well, yeah. This is just another meeting tonight." The man sounded shaken. He also sounded as if he were lying. Zac had heard a lot of people lie.

"And you're assigned to watch the door. How many people are due tonight?"

"The usual."

Zac let the knife sink in a little deeper. "How many?" he repeated very calmly.

"Seven in all, counting me and the honcho who's supposed to show up. I swear it. Seven."

"And how many are already in the house?"

"Five. The special guy isn't here yet."

"Fine," said Zac. "I think I'm beginning to get the picture. A few more questions and this will all be over."

"But I don't know anything else," the man protested. "I keep telling you, I'm just the doorman and this is just a private religious thing."

"You'd be surprised at how much inside information your average doorman picks up in the course of his nightly work."

Guinevere was making slow but steady progress on the ropes. Mason was huddled next to her in the darkness, unable to be of any real assistance but doing his best to provide moral support when the door above the basement stairs opened. Instantly Guinevere froze as a nameless dread went through her. From sheer instinct both she and Mason pretended to be still unconscious.

In the oblong patch of dim light above the stairs she could see the shadowed outline of a figure in a cowled robe. The man's face was in total darkness. He paused to light the candle he held in his hand and then he came slowly, majestically, down the steps. He was followed by a smaller figure, also dressed in a robe, and then the door closed again.

The flickering flames of the candle guided the two newcomers down the steps and over to the altar. Guinevere wondered why no one was using a flashlight. Maybe it didn't fit the image.

The figures talked in subdued tones to each other as they moved around the altar, setting up two more candles in tall black candlesticks. They paid no attention to Guinevere or Mason, who huddled, unmoving, on the floor a few feet away. The light of the candles was barely enough to reach their feet.

A heavy metal bowl was set at the head of the long stone table. Beside it a huge knife with a curved blade was set. Guinevere shivered. She felt rather than heard Mason catch his breath.

"All is ready?" The voice was definitely Baldric's. There was an unnatural formality about the words.

"It is ready. Soon the ceremony may begin," responded Valonia in oddly serene tones. "We will start when the last of them arrive."

"He will be here tonight," Baldric told her. "He says it is time he revealed himself to us. The hour has arrived."

"Excellent. We owe him much. His guidance has been invaluable. It has made all the difference. The Dark Power will be pleased."

"It is especially fitting tonight. The ultimate sacrifice is finally ready. We have been a long time preparing."

Baldric turned his cowled head toward Guinevere and Mason. The flame of the candle cast a long, evil light over his features for a brief moment. In that moment Guinevere was certain she saw madness on the face of another human being. She was assimilating the horror of it when both Valonia and Baldric turned away to fetch a large canvas out of the shadows near the staircase. She couldn't see the painting, but it didn't take much effort to guess that it was

Glare. The painting was hauled over near the altar. It was obviously scheduled to be part of the ceremony.

The door at the top of the stairs opened again. Slowly a parade of three cowled figures came down the steps. They filed into the basement in eerie silence, guided by the candles on the stone table. The door closed with awful finality. The robed figures moved to stand in a small semicircle, and then they began to hum.

For some reason Guinevere thought the tuneless humming was the worst of all. It made no sense. It grated on the ears. It rasped against her nerves. And it never stopped. She wanted to scream. Instead she went back to work with the glass shard. At least the cowled figures were ignoring her and Mason for the time being. The black shadows hid her efforts. She was almost through the rope now. She didn't want to think of how little good all the effort might do. The odds of her and Mason getting out of this room alive were depressingly slim. She wondered what Zac was thinking about her long absence. More importantly, what was he doing about it?

The humming continued for what seemed an endless length of time, and then the door at the top of the stairs opened once more. The noise of the humming rose several notches as another robed figure appeared above the small crowd in the basement. Slowly the other figure started down. Behind him another cowled figure closed the door and came down the steps.

Baldric's voice rose above the humming. "Welcome, my lord," he said gravely to the first man as he reached the bottom of the steps. Baldric didn't pay any attention to the last figure, who took a place at the edge of the circle.

The new figure did not respond, but he inclined his head in regal acceptance of Baldric's words.

"We would have you stand at the head of the altar, my lord." Baldric lifted his arms, and the humming crowd parted to allow the honored figure to move toward the far end of the stone table.

Then Valonia stepped toward the heavy metal bowl and dipped a flaming candle into the center. With a flash of light and a sharp, crackling sound, flames leapt into existence in the bowl.

Guinevere felt her hands come free at that moment. A sob of relief almost escaped her. She touched Mason's arm. He started and then moved his bound arms slightly so that she could reach his ropes.

Around the altar the ceremony began. The humming ceased as Baldric led his small audience in a chorus of strange phrases repeated in an even stranger language. It was obvious that the silent man who stood at the far end of the altar was a special participant. Guinevere remembered what Baldric and Valonia had said earlier about his arrival. This was someone they had never met in person and who was here tonight to reveal himself for the first time.

The dark proceedings continued. The responses of the cowled figures grew louder and a fierce, morbid excitement filled the air. Someone struck a harsh note on a brass gong. At one point *Glare* was lifted up onto the altar and slashed with ritualistic motions.

Guinevere didn't want to think about what was going to be put on the altar after the painting had been dealt with. She was going to have to do something quickly. These people were working themselves up into a frenzy of some sort. Given the presence of the naked blade near the bowl of fire, she could just imagine what was scheduled to happen. The bonds around Mason's wrists came free just as Valonia lifted the knife and passed it through the fire. Baldric started a new, more menacing litany. Guinevere's hands closed around the hem of the black velvet curtain. Silently she guided Mason's fingers to the fabric. When she tugged suggestively at the velvet a few times, he got the message.

Baldric lifted his arms high into the air and called out something totally incomprehensible. Then he whirled and pointed at Guinevere and Mason.

"We will begin with the woman. Bring her forth!"

Two cowled figures detached themselves from the circle and moved forward. Guinevere's hands tightened around the hem of the drape. It would have to be now or never.

"Freeze." Zac's voice cut through the horrifying scene with the impact of a grenade, shattering the awful illusion. "I will shoot whoever moves. And then I will kill your honorable guest attendee. Is that very clear to each and every one present?"

Every cowled head in the room swung around to stare at Zac, who had thrown back his hood. He had his arm around the guest's throat, and even in the flickering firelight it was quite possible to see the wicked looking Beretta in his other hand. For the span of a few seconds stunned silence prevailed. Zac took command, pointing the Beretta at Baldric. "Back against the wall. First you, Baldric, and then the others. Move."

"This is impossible. You can do nothing. You'll never get out of here alive." But Baldric inched slowly backward.

Guinevere, her feet still tied, struggled frantically with her remaining bonds. Mason was doing the same.

"Zac," Guinevere called in breathless relief, "I'm almost out of these ropes. Just a few more seconds."

"As soon as you and Adair are free, get over here."

"We're on our way, Zac." She tugged violently at the ropes.

"No! I will not allow this. You insult and mock the Dark Powers and you shall not escape!" Valonia's voice was a scream of rage.

"Wait, don't do anything," yelled a new voice. It was the man Zac was holding hostage. "Let them all go. He'll kill me. He means it."

"The Dark Powers will protect you if you have served

them as faithfully as you claim!" Valonia yelled back. She lifted the knife in her hand.

"She's right!" Baldric screamed. "Take him. Rush the fool. He cannot stand against all of you at once. *Take him.*"

There was a stumbling, awkward movement from the other figures, a couple of which had been trying to sidle toward the steps.

"I mean it," Zac said with startling calm. "I will kill the first one who tries."

It was Valonia who moved. Seizing the long, curved knife, she whirled toward Mason, who was still struggling with his ropes. In that moment the others seemed to gather their courage. There was a concerted rush, not toward Zac but toward the door. In the resulting confusion Zac was denied a clear shot at Valonia. But Baldric's hand came out of the depths of his robe holding an automatic. Firelight flickered on the short barrel, and Zac caught sight of the gleaming metal. He fired. Baldric screamed and fell backward.

The man Zac was holding tried to dart away in the chaos. Zac used the heel of his hand on the man's jaw, and the figure crumpled to the floor.

Even as she heard Baldric's scream, Guinevere saw Mason twist away in an effort to protect himself, his face a mask of shock and fear. She couldn't reach Valonia in time, and neither could Zac.

"Valonia, stop!" Guinevere pulled furiously on the heavy velvet drapes. They tumbled down in a cascade of thick, smothering fabric, blanketing Valonia, Guinevere, and Mason in a dusty shroud.

"Gwen!"

"In here, Zac." Guinevere shoved at the heavy drapes, emerging at last just as Zac reached her. There was a steady, thudding sound on the stairs as the escaping ceremony attendees made for the only exit.

Zac threw Guinevere a quick glance as he hauled the drapes off Mason and Valonia. She looked all right, and so did Mason. Valonia lay on the cold floor, screaming curses. The knife was not in sight. It had apparently been knocked from her grasp by the falling weight of the drapes.

"Hurry," Zac muttered as he cut Mason's ropes. "For Pete's sake, Gwen, get moving!"

"What's that smell? Zac! Something's on fire."

"The drapes."

Guinevere glanced around and saw the flames from the metal bowl licking hungrily at the edge of the fabric. Already they were throwing huge shadows across the room. In the fiery light she could see two still figures besides Valonia's on the floor.

"Mason, you and Gwen see if you can get Valonia up the steps. If you can't, don't worry about her. I'll see if these other two are in any shape for a little exercise. Hurry, damn it. We haven't got much time."

Guinevere and Mason grabbed Valonia. She didn't fight them. She was too busy sobbing and cursing to unseen powers who had clearly let her down severely.

"It's all right," Guinevere said to Mason. "I can handle her. Help Zac."

"Right." He turned away to give Zac a hand with Baldric and the other robed man.

A few seconds later, smoke licking at their heels in choking, billowing clouds, Guinevere, Mason, and Zac made it safely up the steps and into the kitchen with their prisoners. Even as they raced out the back door the flames found the wooden steps.

By the time Zac had pounded on Abby Kettering's door and gotten her to call the fire department and the police, the Sandwick house was engulfed in flames.

In the violent glare of the burning house Mason Adair stared in stunned amazement at the face of the man who had been the honored guest at the ugly ceremony. It was his cousin, Dane Fitzpatrick.

Chapter Ten

The postmortem was held the following afternoon at one of Pioneer Square's sidewalk taverns. Two glasses of white wine, one beer, and one tequila were ordered. Guinevere, Zac, Carla, and Mason faced each other around the table. Mason still looked dazed.

"I still can't believe Dane flipped out like that," Mason said for about the hundredth time. "I mean, I never really liked the guy, but I didn't know he was nutty."

Zac wrapped his large hand around the tiny tequila glass. "People tend to flip out and get very nutty when big money is at stake."

"But how did you realize Dane was behind the whole thing?" Mason demanded.

"Partly the timing and partly the fact that there was too much money floating around. It was just too damn much of a coincidence that someone was shelling out fifty-five grand in cash for the old Sandwick place right around the time private investigators were asking questions about it and you. Add to that the fact that Dane knew where you were at least six months ago but didn't bother to contact you until this week." Zac paused for another swallow of his drink. "The way I figure it, he couldn't believe his lucky stars when you and your father quarreled and you got yourself stricken from the will. All of a sudden Fitzpatrick was your father's heir, potentially several times richer than he ever dreamed he'd be."

"But," said Guinevere, "that money was going to come to him only if your father died before you and he reconciled. Dane had to live with the knowledge that there was always the possibility that you and your father would repair the breech. It must have made him very nervous."

Zac nodded. "And then one day your father said he was going to try to find you. Dane knew disaster had struck. He decided the only thing he could do was find you, himself, and see that you suffered an unfortunate accident. He very graciously told your father that he would handle the details of hiring a private detective agency and putting them on your trail. Which he did. You weren't hard to find."

Mason shrugged. "I wasn't trying to hide. I just hadn't contacted Dad or the family."

"Fitzpatrick located you about six or seven months ago. In the course of their investigations the agency Dane had hired found out about the Sandwick house and the group you were associating with when you were holding your parties there. They probably pursued that route a while just to see if you were still involved. It would have been mentioned in the report to Fitzpatrick. Later they came up with an address for you. They probably also gave your cousin the incidental information on Barry Hodges, alias Baldric."

Mason sipped his beer thoughtfully. "They turned all the information over to my cousin, who didn't bother to tell my father."

"Exactly," Zac said. "Then he started wondering what sort of accident you might be inclined to suffer out here on the wild and wooly West Coast. Everyone back East knows we're only partially civilized here. The idea of having you perish during some grim occult ceremony appealed to him. For one thing your death couldn't be traced back to him. You had been a member of the group at one time, and as far as anyone might know, you still were. After all, it was a very secret organization. Furthermore, if you were to die because of being associated with a group like that, it would prove to your father that you really had gone off the deep end. It would strengthen Fitzpatrick's position as sole heir."

"But how did he know that the new members of the group were for real?" Carla asked quickly. "There are a lot of strange societies with odd rituals. Most of them harmless. How could Fitzpatrick have found out that Baldric and Valonia really believed in their idiotic rituals and might go in for something like human sacrifice?"

"He didn't at first. He was simply checking out various possibilities. With the information the investigators dug up for him he was able to contact Barry Hodges, or Baldric as he calls himself. The cops told me that he and Valonia, or Valerie Martin, which is her real name, were living in a downtown flophouse at the time. After they started taking cash from your cousin, they moved out and covered their tracks."

"So Dane offered them money and they went for it?" Mason asked.

"Even leaders of insane occult societies need cash. Stone altars and private, soundproof basements don't come cheap," Zac reminded him. "As soon as Fitzpatrick contacted them, he knew he could manipulate them. He took precautions, of course. He was always just a voice on the phone who claimed to be an even more powerful witch or warlock or whatever than either Baldric or Valonia. When he told them the money was being provided by the Dark Powers, they were happy enough to believe him. After your friends split, Baldric and Valonia had picked up new members for their little club. Barry Hodges told Fitzpatrick that they were illegally using the Sandwick house for their ceremonies and were afraid of being caught and kicked out. Once he'd heard about the house and the basement, Fitzpatrick knew it would be perfect for what he had in mind. It was worth fifty-five grand in cash. He saw the purchase as an investment in his own future, so he bought the place for them. But he didn't want Baldric and Valonia living there until after his goal was accomplished. They might have drawn too much attention to themselves and ruined everything. So Fitzpatrick made it a condition that Baldric and Valonia and their cute little group had to remain as anonymous and mysterious as possible. After six months of taking his money they were ready to go along with Fitzpatrick when he suggested that the way to become as rich and powerful as he was—"

"Was to have a human sacrifice," Carla concluded with a shudder.

"Something like that," Zac agreed. "If it hadn't worked, Fitzpatrick would have arranged some other kind of accident for Mason."

"But why did he attend the ceremony last night?" Mason asked. "Why not stay safely on the East Coast?"

"As far as your family is concerned, he was on the East Coast, supposedly vacationing briefly at his country home." Zac gave Mason a level glance. "He came to the ceremony because he wanted to make absolutely certain that the whole plan had worked. He wanted you dead, and he didn't want any slipups or surprises. Murderers tend to be obsessively thorough about the job. They might make a hundred other mistakes in the course of the crime, but they don't want to screw up the act of murder itself. He never intended to reveal himself after the ceremony, of course. He was simply going to disappear, leaving his little gang to figure out how to get rid of the body and what to do next. They were stupid enough, so they probably would have been caught eventually. But they couldn't point the finger at him. The cops would assume that the mysterious 'voice' that had told them to perform the sacrifice was just another manifestation of their craziness. But Fitzpatrick had told Baldric and Valonia that he would reveal himself after the ceremony. He had promised them that afterward they would be part of the Inner Circle or some such nonsense."

"Why did they grab Gwen?" Carla demanded, glâncing worriedly at her sister.

"Because she was getting too involved in the things that were happening to Mason. And she actually saw Baldric that night Mason walked in on him in the studio. Baldric had gone there to deface another painting. He saw it as part of the ritual of preparation for the sacrifice. Baldric's one talent seems to be a certain ability with locks. Mason surprised him. Baldric panicked and slugged him. Then he looked out through the studio window and saw Gwen staring at him from her kitchen window. He and Valonia tried to warn her off—"

"The broken mirror!" Guinevere stared at Zac.

He nodded once, very grimly. "Exactly. The broken mirror. But she was a witness and appeared to be close to Mason. So in the end Baldric and Valonia convinced themselves that she had to be part of the sacrifice. I don't think Fitzpatrick knew until he showed up in the Sandwick basement last night that she was on the agenda, along with Mason. Baldric and I tangled because I surprised him while he was trying to hide *Glare.*"

"Why did Dane bother to look me up at all this past week?" Mason asked curiously.

Zac shrugged. "It was a stupid move on his part and was probably connected with the obsession that made him want to be present at the ceremony. Something to do with the hunter playing with his prey. It's hard to explain, but I've seen people do it on more than one occasion." Zac paused and then said very quietly, "I've done it myself."

"Last night when you realized we'd been kidnapped, what made you head first for the Sandwick place?" Mason asked.

"It was the logical point at which to start. If there had

been no sign of you there, I would have called in the cops and anyone else I could think of because, frankly, there was no other place to start looking." Zac finished the tequila in one long, heartfelt gulp. "It shouldn't be tough for the cops to find the ones who got away last night. Baldric and Valonia will talk their heads off."

"While my cousin hires the best lawyer money can buy. Probably someone from the family firm," Mason finished wryly.

"That reminds me," Carla said slowly. "The first stories have already appeared in this morning's paper. So far I've kept Mason under wraps. The press hasn't located him yet, but it won't be long. The same goes for Gwen. I think we should hold a little war council to decide how we're going to handle this. There's no way to keep it quiet."

"So much for trying to prevent gossip and scandal," Guinevere said with a sigh. "I'm sorry, Mason."

Carla lifted her chin, the light of excitement in her eyes. "Don't worry about it. The way I have it figured, we can work the whole mess to the advantage of Mason's career. I've already contacted that reporter from the *Review-Times* who wanted to talk to Mason about his art. I've promised him the inside scoop on this sacrifice story. He's thrilled. Art and music always get pushed to the second or third section of the paper. They're almost never considered front-page material. This is his chance at the big time. He's never gotten to do a front-page story before. Don't worry about the publicity. In this day and age any publicity is good publicity, if it's handled correctly. By the time I get finished handling this, Mason's going to be the hottest artist in the state. Maybe on the whole West Coast. We can generate all kinds of excitement."

Guinevere, Zac, and Mason stared at her. Finally Guinevere asked hesitantly, "Carla, are you sure you know what you're doing?"

"Positive." She jumped to her feet and reached for Mason's arm. "Come on, Mason. We need to go practice exactly what you're going to say to the reporter."

Mason grinned, obviously willing to let her take the lead. "What about Gwen?"

"Oh, I think we can keep Gwen out of this," Carla said easily. "You're the main story. Gwen will just show up as a small footnote if we handle this right."

"Mason," Guinevere said urgently as the other two prepared to depart, "did you . . . did you call your father?"

His grin faded. "This morning. I had to tell him about Dane first. I didn't want him finding out secondhand."

"How did it go? The conversation with your father, I mean," she pressed.

Mason's mouth curved faintly. "Let's just say I'm flying back East in a week or so to renew my acquaintance with my family. We'll take it from there."

"Take them one of your paintings," Zac suggested mildly.

"I'll do that. Oh, and by the way, I don't want you to think I'm not going to pay my tab. I owe Free Enterprise Security, Inc. my life. I haven't got a lot of cash on hand yet, but I've got a couple of paintings you might like. Theresa tells me that in the current market they're probably worth fifteen hundred apiece. Will that cover the bill?"

"More than cover it," Zac said with a grin. "I'll hang them in my office. I need a better view."

Zac and Guinevere watched the other two walk arm in arm down the street. For a long time silence hovered over the table. Then Zac pushed aside his empty glass.

"Ready to go home?"

"Yes."

Neither said anything else during the short walk up the street to Guinevere's apartment. But when Zac opened the door, he said quietly, "You know, I've kind of gotten used to this place."

"Have you?" Guinevere walked into her brightly

colored living room and tossed down her shoulder bag. "I've kind of gotten used to having you around." She smiled tremulously and turned away to gaze out the window at the street below. A mother and two toddlers were waiting for the bus. Zac came to stand behind Guinevere, one hand on her shoulder. He looked down at the small family.

"Cute kids." His voice was perfectly neutral.

Guinevere took a deep breath. It was time to ask. "Zac, have you been trying to tell me something lately?"

He frowned. "About what?"

"About children." She stood very still. "I need to know, Zac. Are you . . . have you decided you want a family? Is that why you've been worrying about biological clocks and babies?"

"What I want," Zac said quietly, "is you."

She let out a long sigh and leaned her neat head back against his shoulder. "But the baby talk . . ."

"I started worrying that you might be thinking about having kids. Every other woman I've run into lately seems to be getting anxious. But you never said anything. I tried to get you to talk about it. I was afraid you'd decide you want them and that I wasn't the right man to be the father." His fingers tightened around her shoulder. "I couldn't stand it if you went out looking for another man to be the father."

"You don't have to worry about that, Zac," she said simply. "Never worry about that."

"Because you don't want kids?"

"I don't have any particular desire for children. Not now. But if I ever do want them . . ." She turned into his arms and lifted her face. "Your genes are the ones I'd go after. I promise."

He relaxed, holding her close. "I'm glad to hear it."

"What about you, Zac?"

"I've told you. What I want is you."

"You don't feel any pressing need to become a father?"

He shook his head, smiling faintly. "No. But if I ever do, your genes are the ones I'll go after."

"Promise?" she asked, nestling against him.

"I swear it. No one else's would do."

"Thank you. I feel much better," she admitted honestly.

"I think," Zac said carefully, "that we've both been a little insecure lately."

"You mean, we've been jealous of each other and worrying that the other person was planning to run off and start a family with someone else."

"Like I said. Insecure." He framed her face between his hands. "Gwen . . ."

"I know, Zac. I love you."

He kissed her, all his own special needs and longing pouring over her. "That's what I've been needing to hear. I love you Guinevere."

For a few seconds they stood there as the evening sun faded outside the window. Then Guinevere said softly, "I'd better shop for a new coffeepot tomorrow."

"New coffeepot, hell. We'll shop for a whole new machine. We'll give the other one to a thrift shop."

"But, Zac, a new machine will cost a lot of money."

"We'll take the money from the petty cash fund of Free Enterprise Security and Camelot Services. The way you use coffee machines and pots, I figure it's a business expense."

Guinevere thought about going shopping for a household appliance with Zac. There was something very pleasantly committed about the whole project. When she looked up at him she knew Zac was thinking the same thing.

Without another word of protest, she put her arms around his neck and kissed him.

Chapter One

Guinevere Jones handed the sniffling young woman another tissue and waited for the newest spate of tears to halt. As she waited, she pushed the cup of tea closer to her companion's elbow, silently urging her to take another sip.

Tea and sympathy. It wasn't much to offer under the circumstances, but until Sally Evenson had composed herself, there wasn't much else Guinevere could do. The two women were seated at the corner table in a small restaurant just off First Avenue in downtown Seattle. It was the middle of August, and the temperature outside was in the mid-seventies. Perfect weather for dining at one of the outside tables, but much too public for poor Sally in her present mood.

Sally Evenson had worked for Camelot Services as a temporary secretary for several months. Guinevere had sent her out on a number of jobs, and the frail-looking Sally had gained confidence and skill with each new assignment. She had been turning into one of Guinevere's most reliable temps until disaster struck on the latest assignment. Guinevere still wasn't certain just what shape disaster had taken because all Sally had been able to do for the past half hour was cry. Perhaps it was time to take a firm hand.

"All right, Sally, finish your tea and tell me exactly what's going on at Gage and Watson."

Sally raised her head, her eyes swollen and red. She was

a young woman—twenty-three, to be exact—painfully thin and rather nervous, even in the most serene situations. Some of that nervousness had been fading lately as Sally's job performance had improved. There had been a direct correlation between confidence and composure. Guinevere had been pleased at the transformation, but now it seemed that all the progress had been undone.

"I can't talk about it, Miss Jones. You wouldn't understand. No one would understand. I'm sorry to bother you like this. I don't know what got into me. It's just that lately everything seems so . . . so impossible." Sally ducked her head into the tissue again and blew her nose. Whatever claim to attractiveness the young woman had was submerged beneath the mournful wariness in her pale blue-green eyes and her tautly drawn features. Her hair was an indeterminate shade of brown worn in a short bob that badly needed a professional stylist's touch. She still wore her Camelot Services blazer, a smartly cut jacket of royal blue with the new Camelot Services crest on the left pocket.

Sally had fallen in love with the blazer the day Guinevere had given it to her. It was probably the most expensive garment she had ever had. Two months ago Guinevere had hit on the idea of giving all her skilled, long-term employees a similar jacket as a symbol of their elite status in the temporary services field. The blazers were slowly but surely becoming an emblem of the best in temporary help in the Seattle business community. Camelot Services employees wore them with pride. It was good advertising, Guinevere told herself each time she wrote out a corporate check for another of the expensive blazers.

Guinevere took a sip of coffee and set the cup down gently but firmly. "Sally, I can't help you if you don't tell me what's going on. Now, it's been obvious for the past couple of weeks that you've developed personal problems. I do not believe in getting involved in my employees' problems unless they affect job performance. Unfortunately, your problem has gotten to that stage. If you don't pull yourself together, I'm going to have to take you off the Gage and Watson job. You know it and I know it."

Sally stared at her with horror. "Oh, please, Miss Jones, don't do that. I love the job, and my manager at Gage and Watson says it could go on for a couple more months. I need the money. I've moved into a new apartment and I was going to go shopping for some clothes and I wanted to buy a new stereo . . ."

"All right, all right," Guinevere said gently, holding up a hand to stem the flow of protest. "I realize you need the job. And I need you on it. You've been doing excellent work. Gage and Watson assures me that they're very pleased. I wouldn't be surprised if, when this assignment is over, they offer you full-time employment."

Sally's face lit up. "Do you really think so? Oh, Miss Jones, that would be fabulous. A real full-time job. A *career.*" For a moment she was lost in blissful contemplation of a future in which she had a career.

Guinevere smiled wryly. "Gage and Watson's gain will be my loss."

Sally's excitement dissolved on the spot. Guiltily she dabbed at her eyes. "Of course. I forgot. If I were to get a full-time job at Gage and Watson, I'd no longer be able to work for you on a temporary basis, would I? I'm sorry, Miss Jones, I didn't stop to think. I owe everything to you. I wouldn't dream of leaving you after all you've done for me."

Guinevere grinned. "You most certainly will leave me when the right full-time position comes along. It's called career advancement, Sally, and although I'll hate to lose you, I have absolutely no intention of holding you back. Don't worry. Happens all the time in the temporary help field. I'm used to it." Which didn't mean she liked it, but she was businesswoman enough to accept the inevitable.

Besides, sending out temps who were good enough to get hired on permanently at the offices where they had worked on a temporary basis was just another example of sound advertising. As she was always telling Zac, you had to look on the positive side.

Sally smiled tremulously. "You're so understanding, Miss Jones."

"I'm trying to be, Sally. I'm trying. Now tell me what's gone wrong at Gage and Watson."

The young woman hesitated and then confided in a rush, "It's got nothing to do with Gage and Watson. Gage and Watson is a wonderful company, Miss Jones."

"Is it the people you're working with? Is some man hassling you on the job? There are laws against that, you know," Guinevere said bluntly.

"Oh, no, nothing like that." Sally gave her a pathetic glance. "I'm not exactly the sort of woman men would hassle on the job, you know."

"No, I do not know. You're an attractive single woman. Unfortunately job harassment occurs even at the best firms. But if it's not the people at Gage and Watson who are causing you problems, what is it? If it's something too personal to talk about to me, then maybe you should consider some counseling, Sally, because whatever it is, it's starting to ruin everything you've been working on so hard for the past few months."

Sally bit her lip. "I . . . I *am* getting counseling, Miss Jones."

Guinevere's eyebrows went up. "You are?"

"Well, of a sort. I mean, Madame Zoltana is a kind of counselor. She's very intelligent and she . . . she sees things, you know? But she's kind of expensive, and lately I've been having to see her a lot." Sally reached for a few more tissues to blot the new flow of tears.

"Madame Zoltana?" Guinevere stared at Sally. "That

doesn't sound like a counselor's name or title. Who on earth is Madame Zoltana?"

"She's a psychic," Sally explained uneasily, not looking at Guinevere. "Several people at Gage and Watson go to her. Francine Bates introduced me to her a few weeks ago. She has a great gift. Madame Zoltana, that is, not Francine. It's absolutely incredible what she can see. She can tell you so many things about your past that sometimes it's frightening."

Sally looked frightened, all right, Guinevere decided abruptly. Frightened and alone in the world. A very scared young woman. "Tell me, Sally, exactly what Madame Zoltana does when you go to see her."

Sally's lower lip trembled. She stared down into her tea cup. "She sees things. She warns you about things that might happen if you aren't careful. Then she . . . she helps you."

"Helps you?"

The young woman nodded bleakly. "She can sometimes change things for you. Things that . . . that might go wrong."

Guinevere swore silently to herself. "And she'll help you avoid these things that might go wrong as long as you continue seeing her on a regular basis, I suppose?"

Sally nodded, looking up with a kind of sad fear in her wet eyes. "I do try to see her regularly, Miss Jones. But, as I said, she's very expensive and last week when I explained to her that I might not be able to pay her fees she said that unless I did, the most awful thing would happen."

"What did she say would happen, Sally?"

Sally Evenson collapsed in tears, and then, a long while later, she told Guinevere exactly what threat hung over her frail, young head.

Guinevere was still fuming when she finally got back to the office an hour later. Trina Hood, the temp Guinevere had used to help out in Camelot Service's own offices, looked up with a cheerful smile.

"Mr. Justis called. He said to remind you that you promised to help him deal with the caterer tonight after work. I think he's getting nervous, Miss Jones."

"Zac hasn't ever given an office reception," Guinevere explained mildly as she sat down at her desk and sifted through a small stack of messages. "He's going through the usual party-giver's panic, wondering if he'll wind up spending a fortune on food and champagne and have no one show up. Did he say what time he wanted to meet me?"

Trina nodded. "He said he'll come by our office to collect you around five."

"Collect me?"

"I think that was the word he used. He instructed me not to let you get away."

Guinevere smiled fondly. "Poor Zac. Amazing how a man with all his talents is reduced to fear and trembling by the mere thought of giving a party. Anything else crucial happen while I was gone?"

"Two more calls for clerks needed for vacation fill-ins. I've already contacted two people in our files. Both said they'd report to work at the firms tomorrow morning."

"Great." Guinevere smiled approvingly at Trina. She had used a handful of different people from her own staff during the past few weeks, experimenting in an attempt to find someone who would work out on a full-time basis. After her sister Carla had left to set up her own art gallery in Pioneer Square, Guinevere had discovered just how much she had come to rely on full-time office help at Camelot Services.

Trina Hood was showing definite potential. She was a pleasant woman in her mid-forties who had recently been divorced and now had two children to raise alone. There was a certain comfortable plumpness about her, and she had an excellent telephone voice. She was also a hard worker and anxious to please. As she had explained to Guinevere, she had been out of the work force for almost ten years and had been terrified of the prospect of having to find a job. She had decided to start out as a Camelot temp in an effort to get her feet wet in the business world. She had walked through the doors of Camelot Services on the very day that Guinevere had acknowledged to herself that she wasn't going to be able to get by with part-time help. Guinevere had grabbed her.

"What about Gage and Watson, Gwen? Want me to find someone to replace Sally Evenson?" Trina asked quietly. She was well aware that things were shaky.

Guinevere thought for a moment. "No," she said finally, "I think I'll go over to Gage and Watson myself for a few days. Something is bothering Sally, and I want to check out the situation there. Can you find her another short-term assignment? She needs to work."

Trina nodded. "Gallinger Industries needs a typist for a few days."

"Put Sally on it."

"I don't get it. You're going to go into Gage and Watson yourself?"

"That's right. I'll tell Gage and Watson that Sally is ill and that I'm her replacement."

"Well, all right, but I don't understand why you want to take one of your own temporary assignments. What about running things here?"

"I shall rely on you, Trina."

Zac showed up in the doorway of Camelot Services at five minutes after five. It was obvious that he had walked straight down the hill from his own small office in a Fourth Avenue high-rise. He had his conservatively tailored jacket hooked over one shoulder. His crisp white shirt fit him well, emphasizing the solid, compact strength of his shoulders and the flat planes of his stomach.

Zachariah Justis, president and sole employee of the firm Free Enterprise Security, Inc., would never win any male beauty contests. The first time Guinevere had met him she had labeled him a frog. It wasn't that he was as ugly as a frog, it was just that he had been surrounded at the time by a bar full of young, beautiful, upwardly mobile types, and in their midst he had stood out quite prominently. Add to that the fact that shortly after he'd introduced himself to Guinevere he'd coerced her into helping him in an investigation and one could understand why she had been less than initially enthusiastic about Zac Justis.

Zac was just under six feet tall, a compactly built man with short, almost military-styled night-dark hair and cool, ghost-gray eyes. He was thirty-six years old, but it had struck Guinevere on occasion that those years must have been hard-fought years of experience. Sometimes she wanted to ask him more about his past, but he usually showed no interest in discussing it, so she tended to back off the subject. Among the few facts she did know was that Zac had spent several years working for a large, multinational security firm before he left it to start his own small business in Seattle.

She could guess at some aspects of his past because she had witnessed some of his more unique skills. She had, for example, seen him make the transition from businessman to cold, lethal hunter on more than one occasion, and it gave her chills to think of the kind of life he must have led before settling down in Seattle. Guinevere still wasn't certain why she had fallen in love with the man. She only knew that her life was never going to be the same now that Zachariah Justis had entered it.

They had begun their relationship as adversaries, but the tension between them had quickly exploded into passion. Passion had led to an affair and to love. It was a very new, cautiously admitted love, something they had both finally acknowledged only a couple months previously. They didn't talk about it very much. There was still a sense of wonder and uncertainty about the relationship as far as she was concerned. In true male fashion, however, Zac seemed to take everything for granted now. That was typical of Zac. He had a blunt, straightforward approach to most things, including, apparently, the matter of falling in love.

Guinevere reminded herself on occasion that there was much she didn't know about Zachariah Justis. In all honesty, the reverse was true too. But Guinevere doubted that a complete résumé of her past would contain any earth-shaking surprises for Zac. Sometimes she wondered what she would learn if she were to see a detailed résumé about him, however. Philosophically she told herself that the early stages of love were a time of discovery. It was not a time to be rushed. She would continue tiptoeing through the forest, feeling her way and learning what she could about Zachariah Justis.

"The caterer said he'd see us at five-thirty," Zac announced as he came through the door. "Let's get going."

"Relax, Zac. He's only a couple of blocks away. We'll get there in plenty of time." Guinevere picked up her shoulder bag and glanced around the office. Trina had left a few minutes earlier. "Besides, I want to talk to you. I need some professional advice."

Zac waited impatiently by the door, his gaze turning suddenly suspicious. "Professional advice? What sort of advice? Gwen, I don't want you getting mixed up in any more crazy investigations. I can find my own clients. I don't need you to dig up more work for me."

She smiled with what she hoped was reassurance. "Calm down. I'm not asking you to take on any investigations. This one I'm going to handle on my own. I just want some advice from you, that's all." She playfully pushed him out into the hall, then locked the office door.

"Gwen, I mean it, I've got enough to do during the next couple of weeks without having to chase after you trying to keep you out of trouble. I've got this damn reception to plan and the move to my new office to supervise. On top of everything else I'm supposed to be interviewing for a secretary. That reminds me. Why haven't you sent anyone over for me to talk to?"

"I'm still selecting the final candidates. A good secretary is hard to find, Zac. It takes time. Trust me."

"Uh-huh. Are you sure you're not being a little too picky?" He took her arm and steered her forcefully down the stairs and out onto the sidewalk.

"Zac, I have to be picky. You're not going to be the easiest man to work for, you know. You need someone calm and unflappable. Someone with a good personality so that she can handle your important clients properly. You also need someone who can do your typing, handle your accounts, and present a good image."

"Damn it, Gwen, I just want a secretary, not a presidential aide."

"Don't worry, Zac. I'll send someone over soon. Now, about my little problem."

"Guinevere, I have learned through hard experience that your problems are rarely *little.*"

"Don't sound so abused. I'm not going to involve you in this. I've told you, I just want some advice. Now, here's the situation. I think one of my employees has become the victim of a very subtle, very cruel protection racket."

Zac slid her a sidelong glance. "Are you kidding?"

"No. Listen to this and tell me what you think. I sent a young woman over to Gage and Watson a few weeks ago."

"The electronics firm?"

Guinevere nodded. "Someone in her office turned her on to a psychic. A character who goes by the name of Madame Zoltana. Madame Zoltana agreed to see her initially for a small consulting fee. But after a couple of visits she revealed to poor little Sally that she knew Sally had gotten pregnant when she was seventeen."

"Oh, hell." Zac sounded as if he knew what was coming.

"Sally was flabbergasted. It seemed to prove that Madame Zoltana really knew her stuff. But it didn't stop there. Zoltana also knew that Sally had given the baby up for adoption. You have to understand, Zac, that the experience nearly devastated Sally. She's a fragile kind of person in the first place. Finding herself pregnant and abandoned at seventeen nearly caused her to commit suicide. She was talked into having the baby by one of those anti-abortion groups. They promised her that once she gave the baby away, she would be free to rebuild her own life. Sally did exactly that. It's been a long, slow process. Because of the baby she was forced to drop out of school. She had to complete high school through a GED program. Her parents disowned her and she was left destitute. It's a long, sad story. Suffice it to say that she's gradually pulled herself back together. A few months ago she came to work for me and she's shown remarkable improvement on the job. She's starting to come into her own at last. I'm very proud of her."

"Guinevere the social worker," Zac commented dryly.

"I'm serious, Zac. That young woman has really started to get her act together during the past few months. For the first time since she was seventeen she's beginning to see a future for herself. But she's still very fragile, Zac. Now along comes this screwy Madame Zoltana and warns her that her whole world is about to fall apart again."

"How?"

Guinevere drew a deep breath. "She told Sally that unless she kept coming to her on a regular basis, the baby she gave away when she was seventeen would someday learn who its natural mother is, come looking for her, and ruin Sally's life. For the right price, Madame Zoltana says, she can prevent that from happening with her psychic powers. Poor little Sally is absolutely terrified."

Zac whistled softly. "I'll be damned. That's pretty grim, all right. What a racket."

"That's exactly what it sounded like to me. A sleazy sort of protection racket. Madame Zoltana finds some useful secret in a person's past and then offers 'protection' for a price."

"And the price is continued visits to Madame Zoltana at very high fees?"

"Exactly." Guinevere lifted her chin determinedly. "I can't allow that sort of thing to happen to one of my employees on the job, Zac. I'm going to find out what's going on and expose the whole sordid mess. That Madame Zoltana deserves to be hung."

Zac sighed. "Gwen, if people are stupid enough to believe in psychics and dumb enough to pay them off, there's just not much you can do about it. About all you can do is explain to Sally what's going on and hope she'll be smart enough to believe you."

"Poor Sally is too distraught to know what to believe. I've got to prove that Zoltana is a fraud."

"Be reasonable, Gwen. How are you going to do that?"

"The way I figure it," Guinevere said thoughtfully, "Zoltana must have some inside help at Gage and Watson. Sally's not the only G and W employee who's seeing her, and from what I can gather a couple of the others have been getting the same treatment Sally has. Somehow Zoltana spots the gullible ones and then finds out something she can use against them."

Zac lifted one brow. "Inside help?"

"Yeah, you know, someone who works at Gage and Watson and gets potential victims to confide in her. She then passes the information along to Zoltana. From what Sally told me today that would seem to be the way things work."

"Gwen, do you mind if I point out that you've got a company to run? You can't make a career out of exposing fraudulent psychics. Believe me, Houdini tried and it didn't do much good. There are always going to be some people who will want to believe in frauds. As long as there are believers, there will be frauds."

"All I want is a little advice from you, Zac. I thought you could give me some pointers on how to go about exposing a fraud."

"As usual," Zac said with a long-suffering sigh, "my advice to you is to stay out of it. But, as usual, I suppose you won't pay any attention."

Guinevere smiled contentedly. "I knew you'd help me."

"Wait a minute, I never said I'd help."

"Now, Zac, I'm approaching you in a professional capacity here."

"The hell you are. You're just trying to get some free assistance," he shot back.

"Well, you owe me something for all the help I'm giving you in planning your reception," Guinevere informed him as they reached the entrance of a trendy, delicatessen-restaurant on Western Avenue. "Here we are. We can discuss my case later. Now remember what I told you about dealing with this caterer, Zac. I don't want you making a fuss every time I mention French champagne or good pâté. If you're going to have a proper reception for your clients, you have to do it right. You can't stint. You must go first-class."

"Easy for you to say. It's not your money."

"Quit complaining. This is going to be a wonderful party. Great PR for Free Enterprise Security."

"What if no one shows up?" he demanded, holding open the door for her.

"Then you and I will have a lot of food and champagne to eat. Might take us the rest of the year."

"Gwen!" Horrified, he hurried after her, catching up

just as she hailed the young chef with whom they had an appointment.

"Hello, Charles," Guinevere said cordially. "I think we're ready to make the final decisions. Zac has made it clear that he wants everything to be just right, so please feel free to advise us." She ignored Zac's groan of despair and led the two men toward a vacant table.

"I am sure you will be quite pleased, Mr. Justis," Charles assured him, taking out a pen and a long pad of paper. "Shall we deal with the canapés and pâtés first? We have an excellent lobster pâté I would like to suggest. It's a speciality of the restaurant and we do it exceedingly well."

"Lobster?" Zac's voice sounded strained. *"Lobster?"*

"I think the lobster is a wonderful suggestion, Charles," Guinevere offered swiftly. "I also think we should feature some salmon, don't you?"

"Salmon is always popular," Charles agreed, scribbling rapidly. "And we do a truly superior salmon hors d'oeuvre that features just a touch of dill and capers. I'm sure you'll like it."

Zac knew there was no room in this conversation for him. He sat back in his chair, watching dolefully as Guinevere blithely ran up the tab for the reception he was planning. Hard to believe that initially it was just an off-the-cuff suggestion he had made when he'd told her he'd decided to move the offices of Free Enterprise Security into a suite higher up in the building where he presently rented a tiny cubicle. Business had been improving for his firm lately, and Zac was anxious to move up in the world. Time to get a real office, a view, and a secretary. One had to think of image. And wouldn't it be nice maybe to invite some of his clients to a little reception to celebrate?

Guinevere had assured him that it was a brilliant notion. The next thing Zac knew, he was planning a no-expense-spared party. The formal announcements had gone out last week. Guinevere had sent a clerk over to help him address the envelopes. After that he was committed. Panic had set in almost at once. Now he was beyond panic. He had placed himself in Guinevere's hands, and Lord only knew what the result would be. One thing was for certain: He was going to be a lot poorer when it was all over.

But that was the thing about Guinevere Jones. Life hadn't been the same for Zac since he had met her. And when all was said and done, he knew he wouldn't ever want to go back to the way things had been before she had entered his world. Zac tended to take a realistic, pragmatic view of life and of himself. He knew himself well enough, for example, to know that he'd do anything to keep Guinevere safe. It was a measure of the differences between them that she would undoubtedly be shocked if she knew that. As far as Zac was concerned, it was just a fact of life.

JAYNE CASTLE lives in Seattle, Washington, with her husband, her bird, and a magnificent water view. She is a connoisseur of good food and wine as well as of mystery, suspense, and adventure fiction. A popular and prolific author, Ms. Castle—who also writes as Stephanie James and Jayne Ann Krentz—currently has over 7 million books in print.

HOW DID YOU LIKE THIS BOOK?

Fill out and mail this questionnaire and you will be helping us to bring you the kinds of books YOU like to read.

1. TITLE OF THIS BOOK:

____

2. TYPE OF BOOK (check only ONE type):

☐ mystery ☐ action/adventure ☐ romance

3. Please indicate how much you liked or disliked certain things about this book.

	liked a lot	liked a little	disliked a little	disliked a lot
the female lead	☐	☐	☐	☐
the male lead	☐	☐	☐	☐
the plot	☐	☐	☐	☐
the romance	☐	☐	☐	☐
the action & adventure	☐	☐	☐	☐
the mystery	☐	☐	☐	☐
the location	☐	☐	☐	☐
anything else you liked or disliked?				
______________	☐	☐	☐	☐
______________	☐	☐	☐	☐

4. Do you think the story had
   - ☐ too much romance
   - ☐ just the right amount of romance
   - ☐ too little romance

5. Would you buy another book in this sequence of novels?

☐ definitely yes ☐ probably yes ☐ probably no ☐ definitely no

6. How did you come to read this book?
   - ☐ I read a book in this sequence before, and I liked it.
   - ☐ I saw it in the store, and it seemed interesting.
   - ☐ Someone told me it was a good book.
   - ☐ Other: ______________________________

7. In the last three months, approximately how many of the following kinds of books have you read?

	0	1-2	3-6	7 or more
mystery/detective	☐	☐	☐	☐
action/adventure	☐	☐	☐	☐
psychological suspense	☐	☐	☐	☐
occult/supernatural	☐	☐	☐	☐
romance series (like Harlequin)	☐	☐	☐	☐
romance (not series)	☐	☐	☐	☐
espionage/spy	☐	☐	☐	☐

8. What are your three favorite television shows?

1. ______________________________

2. ______________________________

3. ______________________________

9. In what year were you born?

____

10. What is your education?

☐ some high school
☐ high school graduate
☐ some college
☐ college graduate
☐ more than college

IF YOU HAVE ANY OTHER COMMENTS YOU WOULD LIKE TO MAKE ABOUT THIS BOOK, PLEASE FEEL FREE. WE WELCOME ANY OF YOUR THOUGHTS.

NAME: ______________________________

ADDRESS: ______________________________

____

PHONE NUMUBER: ______________________________

Please put this questionnaire in a stamped envelope and mail it to:

Reader Research Program
Dell Publishing Co.
245 East 47th Street
New York, NY 10017

Thank You.

BE